About the Author

Ricardo Ben-Oliel was born in Portugal, in 1944, in the former Portuguese colony, Cape Verde, where his mother's family found refuge during the Nazi period. In 1973, for ideological reasons, he immigrated to Israel. After getting a law doctorate from the Hebrew University of Jerusalem, he began an academic career. Nowadays, he is a full professor (emeritus) at the University of Haifa, Faculty of Law. Beyond this novel, he published three short story books. Eminent Portuguese writers and critics have praised all of his literary work; it was referred to in radio and television programs nationwide.

Jerusalem, the Cry!

Ricardo Ben-Oliel

Jerusalem, the Cry!

Olympia Publishers
London

www.olympiapublishers.com
OLYMPIA PAPERBACK EDITION

Copyright © Ricardo Ben-Oliel 2024

The right of Ricardo Ben-Oliel to be identified as author of
this work has been asserted in accordance with sections 77 and 78 of
the Copyright, Designs and Patents Act 1988.

All Rights Reserved

No reproduction, copy or transmission of this publication
may be made without written permission.
No paragraph of this publication may be reproduced,
copied or transmitted save with the written permission of the publisher,
or in accordance with the provisions
of the Copyright Act 1956 (as amended).

Any person who commits any unauthorised act in relation to
this publication may be liable to criminal
prosecution and civil claims for damage.

A CIP catalogue record for this title is
available from the British Library.

ISBN: 978-1-80439-672-8

First Published in 2024

Olympia Publishers
Tallis House
2 Tallis Street
London
EC4Y 0AB

Printed in Great Britain

Dedication

To my grandparents Richard and Hedwig Neumann, my heroes.

Acknowledgements

I feel deeply indebted to my son Daniel. Without his initiative and personal encouragement, this book wouldn't have been translated and published.

Is there a belief, gesture or words, a fear, laughter or cry that is unique, exclusive, genuinely mine, or is everything in me nothing more than a replica, belonging to all of you, especially to those who are no longer here?

CONTENTS

Neguev	15
In the Kibbutz	19
That's How I Met You, Dana	52
Coming Back	57
Your House, Dana	70
My Home	86
Judaism – A Brief Note	115
Jerusalem, the Cry!	132
Lisbon Reinvented	139

I

Neguev

She had been silent at my side for some time, while the car snuck down the deserted hill. Behind the dark lenses, her gaze would not be discovered, it was no use insisting, nor did her sphinx-like posture let us foresee the enigma that was inside her.

Nor could she guess what I was saying to myself; "I always dreamed that one day you would come, Dana; that has happened, and this is the moment. I have longed to run through the desert with you. Who knows, perhaps even to live there, but today it is the desert that appeals to us, forcing us to be silent, because the silence is also the desert's speech."

Suddenly, Dana interrupted to find out how much distance was left. She traced her leg, aligned her body at a brief angle toward me, her lips ajar inviting me to penetrate.

It was afternoon when we arrived in Mitzpé Ramon. From the terrace of the Bereshit Hotel, where a pool of blue water shimmered, the Negev, immense and golden, smiled with its bare breasts and thousand-year-old craters, kissing mouths with which the gods said goodbye before leaving forever.

It took no time before Dana, in a leap, awoke the warm, refulgent water of the pool; then it was me who dove in. Soon, we found ourselves in one embrace.

We loved each other with the eagerness of a time gone

by, a time lost, not forgotten. We were one body, we spoke our secret speech that repeated itself, renewed itself.

Dana turned her olive-green gaze to me, and told me, "I was afraid you wouldn't want me, Alan. I accepted even if you hated me, for I'm sure you would have thought I had once betrayed you. And you wouldn't be short of reasons to judge. But, perhaps, it's not too late to tell you that I didn't."

I let Dana speak, without interrupting her. The cool, white Golan wine freed us from the last shred of awkwardness that was holding us back, so I heard her words flow like long-contained waters, eager to be released.

"Alan, it's important to me that you know this; you've always lived with me, you've never stopped being by my side, even you don't know it…"

"But, unexpectedly, it was a male voice that came to answer the phone, and you, Dana, didn't show up, and that without you giving me any explanation."

"It's hard to tell you how hard it was for me. To see someone I didn't love – a cousin who, taking advantage of the situation, started coming to our house and ruin the best part of my life, which was us… But if I allowed it, Alan, and if I even asked him to do it, it was only for you, hard as it may seem. The accident, Alan, the crash in just a few seconds, and everything changed. My father will have died instantly; mother with a terrible diagnosis, paraplegic for the rest of her life; Lilucha, with a skull fracture, between several others. I could not abandon them. Do you know – and you experienced it too – what it is like? Suddenly, your world begins to collapse, to fall apart completely, without you having any possibility of avoiding it, or even of minimizing the collapse?"

"I'd be ready to come back, Dana, come back to you,

accompany you in any way I could. But I saw that you didn't want me, because I find a male voice on the phone, that doesn't call you, that pushes me away..."

"It was cruel of me," she admitted, "I'll give you that, but believe me, Alan, I did it for you. I had no doubt you'd come back, that's what I wanted to avoid. You were at the beginning of your project, it was impossible to let it go, and I would never forgive myself for bringing down your life's dream, the *aliah*, the going to Israel. All your experiences and memories that we talked about so often combined for you to leave one day. Your own home prepared you for a world where only in the heterogeneity of habits and cultures did you find your balance. In your daily life, you lived the horror of the *Shoah*, the inhumanity of wars, the silent suffering of those around you. I never forgot what you used to tell me about your experience when you visited the kibbutz where you met your cousins – a true saga, full of vigour and love for life – and then the return, the nightmare that was the return to the Salazar swamp, to the stinginess of its values, of which you were well aware in your provincial court. Even in my house, Alan, you were a stranger. That's how you felt, no matter how much we did to avoid it; I'm telling you now, my parents looked at you with sympathy, they even recognized the strength of your convictions. It was you, Alan, who was not there. I didn't hesitate to say that you would return, only I couldn't allow it. You started to build your true world very early, at school, in religion classes. Later, with that enthusiasm, you dedicated yourself to the values of Judaism, and what you told me about all that, Alan! And as you well know, I also fell in love with your ideals, I saw myself taking part in your project, how enticing it seemed to me, what an extraordinary challenge awaited us both! Then there was the horror of the accident, and I could no longer leave the house. My mother survived, but in a total dependence on me. You ask about the present situation, after all these years. Lilucha made a full recovery. My mother passed away a short while ago."

Frames of a memory. Snapshots that are, sometimes, other short films of a past that merge in the dark of time – always infinitesimal moments of a life that by magical force will last, their true origins go back to the threshold of days.

Memories in which you, Dana, and many others participated – who and for what obscure reasons? – extras, who later departed, unaware of the miraculous trail that was yours.

Brief windows that open and limit our freedom to be other, humus of our beliefs, belongings and loves, the reason even for how much has passed us by, remaining unattended.

Memories that are mine, yours, ours, even the cry that once exploded in you, Dana; bound in shackles we remain, powerless. Why this, that one and not another fragment of memory, if all already tinged by the watercolour of time? What acuity will they have in days to come, but above all what is the reason for the choice, for the election of one and more images that will never leave us? The enigma will endure, Dana. Therein lies its beauty.

II

In the Kibbutz

October 1967, in the aftermath of the Six-Day War, somewhere in Galilee

There are those moments when the breadth of the world is confined to very little, is reduced to one, almost nothing. That's what happened that day. All I could see was the tongue of the road that the glass of the bus was swallowing up, the back of the driver and his sweater pulled up to his neck. Right at the start, I had told him my destination, with the request that he not forget to tell me where to get off. So, after a while, certainly not long enough, I waited anxiously for his hand signal to alert me. In those moments, nothing else mattered. Until the warning came. After hours of travel, the driver had his arm outstretched to the side, gesticulating frantically to say that he would soon be at the next stop. He immediately made the bus move fast and snore loudly – the noise would be in tune with the throbbing inside me – as if he wanted to get rid of me. That was how it seemed to me.

Looking around, there was not a soul, not a house in sight. Vehicles were rare. A sudden fear of being abandoned somewhere else, in no man's land. By now, the car was rattling, losing speed, until it stopped, sniffling. Again, the insistent squinting of the driver, now telling me it was right there. To hurry me along. *Maher*! In a near leap, I' was out the door. I shook for no reason. I looked at the road of a brilliant black, silent and slender. On one side, eucalyptus trees covered with a thick branching, baroque robes from the ground to the top – in order to conceal, so I was told, the fighting-cars and others that would not be – on the other, the sad platoon of cypress trees, in their pointed and sombre green.

From the bus that had left, shortly after, there was nothing but a silent stain blurring into the blue. Becoming a dark dot until it faded away altogether.

I found myself twisted by a fierce restlessness, an almost regret. Standing there, the bag spilled on the floor, I wondered why I had come. What was waiting for me? Was there any point in such a gathering of relatives; she, my mother's cousin, plus husband and a child daughter, relatives I knew little or nothing about? Would they be happy to receive me or would they start counting the days before I left? I can still hear myself carrying on this dialogue inside me, which suddenly ended with the fast and noisy escape of a passing car. As there was nothing more to be done, I went on.

A few metres up the road, I came across a gate. It would have to be there. I went through it. I felt my footsteps on the rough earth. But I was now inside. I began to be a part of. A little light of hope lit up for me, without my knowing what for. I went on. At the reception of the kibbutz, I met two faces that stared at me.

They heard from me a tactless information, plus the family name. That I should wait. The detachment with which they looked at me made me resent the irrelevance of my presence and of myself. But it had the power to serenade me.

It didn't last until it was you coming closer, coming to meet me. In a quiet, short, slightly dragging walk. Seeing you, you were almost my mother. The same height. The blue, worn, almond gaze. A silent, laughing presence. You looked at me with your old face that I had seen nowhere before and with the maturity of one who knows me. Then there was no more reason for the embrace, we held hands and you took me away.

After a very short time, you would die. I was still given the time to hear you. I remember you. When I returned home, it was Larry who wrote to inform me. Succinctly he did so, for that was his way of saying.

It was necessary to meet you. I had already learned a little from what my mother had told me about you, Gretel. Of holidays spent, with your sister Ruth too, on Grandmother Henriette's farm. Of your antics and the old lady's kindly rants. The rides in grandfather's buggy, the games and races in the forest, the jumps in the lake, the ice-skating. Then, my mother said, the curtain fell, there were years of running away, of scattering, times of silence, until one day, occasionally, she came to know about you, about your address in the kibbutz. The two of them began to correspond from time to time.

You have achieved, Gretel, what not everyone else has been able to achieve: Palestine. You arrived alone. Astonished, wounded of the world. Landed in a port of fragile shelter, on the eve of a new war, always the war. You were left with the kibbutz. There they took you in and you met Larry. Tall, broad-shouldered. A soldier who had been a poet, he had left his verses scattered in newspapers. Having become an authority, he came to offer you the security you so desperately needed.

Yes, it was Larry who gave the news. You never told me

what tormented you, the cancer that gnawed at you, so that without worry I could enjoy those days spent together. Our meeting was good, Gretel. Necessary, decisive even in the future that was opening up to me.

Almost immediately, the conversation turned to the destroyed family and the few who survived, scattered throughout the world. You were in closer contact with your sister Ruth, she had stayed in Prague, but both had no means to visit each other. All that remained were letters. Without encouragement, you asked me – and the question remained with me forever – if it wouldn't be better to shut up, to try to forget, to remake what was left of life.

Notwithstanding the memories, Gretel, happy you seemed to me to have visited you. I think I saw in your sweet and weary eyes the glimmer of a fragile contentment.

You died soon after. You were almost my mother.

I let myself sleep until late. In the morning, I became aware of the bed and the iron closet, of the modesty of the room, of the construction in a blue wood, in strips. It was on such premises that the kibbutz received the child soldiers returning from the units, and whoever else came to visit.

Gretel came for me, took me to her home.

One would suddenly enter the small room. There a furniture that was only fit to be, without adornment or fetish, manufactured in the kibbutz itself, as I was told. A rectangular table with chairs at the sides, another shorter, circular, with three armchairs around it. A little away, still one, rocking. Against the wall, a bookcase, books, total absence of knick-knacks. Just a black and white photograph of the three –

Gretel, Larry, Ronit – sitting by the round table where my cousin and I were meeting. Still a large window that allowed us to see outside, at full length, a row of ruddy geraniums. Absolute minimalism. A *quantum satis*. A simple place where only true speech was desirable.

We were having a frugal breakfast when the door of the house began to be dragged open, then slammed shut. A school bag was thrown to the floor. Her. In her seven, eight years. Short, tousled, dark hair. Big, bright brown eyes. A round face. Ronit.

Ronit stared at me. She did it quickly, then became disinterested. She went to the *kitchenette*, opened the fridge, closed the fridge, searched the cupboards. Gretel, her voice faint, asked a few questions. She excused herself and left to prepare her daughter's meal.

A few minutes and the child was back. Ronit noisily chewed an apple. In between, the mother's soft voice, systematically cut off by some refusing, irrepressible *lô*. Until Ronit sat down to a light meal. She had come to spend *Shabbat* with her parents, after which she would return to the children's dormitory. I let slip the question about the violence of the regime, to which Gretel answered me. First with her silence, then with her hands raised in the air, saying, "What can we do if this is the kibbutz, if we have to clean the streets, look after the clothes and the roses, help with the accounts, especially since they have opened the furniture factory – luckily, we no longer have to milk the cows and climb the orange trees – what can we do, Alan?"

Ronit listened attentively to us, without understanding what we said in a soft, almost musical German, as I always heard my mother say. She didn't hide her curiosity, then her anxiety, when she found a small package next to me. I was also waiting for the moment when I would give her the little *varina*, a traditional fish vendor I had brought. How could I know that she collected dolls from the world, Ronit must have asked. Then she took it from me, already without looking at me. Still two or three more *lô*. She left.

In the middle of the afternoon, Larry arrived. Large in stature. A veteran of the kibbutz. He clutched an enormous pipe, which I later came to know was almost a part of his clothing. He calmly settled in the armchair, rocking. It didn't last until he cut the silence he himself had created, to tell me of Gretel's joy at my coming. And of his pleasure, of course. He spoke between empty spaces. Sometimes, he seemed not to be. Until it occurred to him to inform me that after *Shabbat*, he would take me to visit the fields and facilities of the kibbutz. Between two puffs, he added that the administration had authorized him to use the only old Renault 4 for a trip around the country. We would leave at the beginning of the week. He said it in the measured, low tone of one who announces something he is not accustomed to do. Gretel had listened to him with a wan smile. Until Larry had gone, somewhat unforeseen, leaving the armchair rocking. We remained, Gretel and I; she meditative.

Strangely for me, Larry had not inquired about the distant family at all.

In the communal dining hall. Friday dinner, *Shabbat* night. They were better groomed, many in starched, white shirts, changed out of their business suits, usually tucked in to bringmouxe. Absence of kipas. The women, too, would have spent a few minutes more on themselves. Two candle-lit candelabras that only those who looked for them with their eyes would discover.

In line. Plastic platters in hand, patiently serving themselves by a long counter. Glances exchanged, a few short *shalom*. I followed Gretel and Larry, I followed Ronit.

An unexpected discomfort touched me. A mist that thickens and invades me. The doubt that had already arisen and persisted. *What are you doing here, what have you come for? Look at yourself and understand how alien you are, and not one of all those who are here. Many do not even see you; you are purely non-existent for them. There will be others to whom your different way will have recalled past experiences, worlds that are no longer. Do you rekindle wounds, remove scabs. Today, a deep chasm separates you, you feel it well, and you will not find an ingenious way to approach it. You come face to face with reality, and you, alone. You release the shirt that suffocates you, breathe in as much as you can, but this does not overcome the stifling breath that annuls you. What did you come for?*

Sitting at the long table, Larry said a little bit about me. Then they looked at me. So that I could follow it, the conversation proceeded in no small amount of strained English. It jumped from one subject to another, then I roused myself. The orange harvest and the volume of roses to be exported, especially with the coming of the end-of-year festivities; the surveillance and nightly rounds of the kibbutz, Uzi in hand, and the urgency of one more accountant; the dry winter, the level of the Kineret declining; the film soon to be shown on the kibbutz and who will be next entitled to a holiday abroad; Amit, violinist, Lisa and Aaron's son, and the success he was having in America, handsome reward for how much the kibbutz had invested in him. And, not least, would the head of the communist party, Vilnay, have something new to say at the conference he would give them that evening?

I looked at myself once again. I repeated that this was a people that didn't have, and for whom the perfumed patches of life were definitely not enough. That tore other paths and in a collective effort of self-restraint remoulded its destinies. I reminded myself that they were the ones I sought, I allowed myself to be attentive to the strong voice that reminded me, then I rested. Gretel smiled at me.

By then, everyone was dispersing. Then a small circle was formed around a short creature in a suit and tie; the only one who had presented himself in such a manner. He was the speaker, Comrade Vilnay, who had just arrived. Among the surroundings, the large figure of Larry.

It was night. I left the dining hall and followed Gretel and Ronit, with her repeated *ló*. I said goodbye, longing to be alone. Every now and then, a golden heading cracked in a cavernous sky, then the rumble of a mad thunderstorm. An angry play of light and darkness.

Sunday morning. I followed Larry. As we approached him, he was telling me about the vast orange grove surrounded by a line of cypress trees. Although in profile, I thought I could see in Larry a big smile; he seemed to me to be another one. He was hitched to his pipe, like a smoke machine releasing circles that vanish in the bright morning. He says of the earth that it was necessary to take care of and fertilize and plant and water until those little orange trees turned into people and gave fruit. Then, the area of the orange grove, in hectares; the production and export volumes; the market, the European prices; the amounts involved, many thousands of lire; the risks, the bad weather, especially if there is hail. I looked at the trees already grown, smiling with fruit, but I admitted that it was only much later that I was able to appreciate the grandiosity of the project, when, in other areas, I came across Lilliputian orchards on land stolen from deserted sands. Then I said to myself that this was the beginning of Larry's work; and the question remains, why is it that we are always late in evaluating the efforts of others? A mistake in perception? Selfishness? Self-defence?

Larry didn't wait for me to ask or comment. He hardly looked at me. I saw myself hitched to the locomotive that drove me, I felt small. But there's no need to be surprised, since we both know that I'm just a young graduate, that my only effort will have been that of having engulfed myself for x number of years in y number of manuals, with a whole film of life unrealized. I touch the reality that I am. It is necessary to feel the light and brief existence that animates us and vibrates in us, that is what I tell myself.

In the distance, I began to glimpse something that intrigued and fascinated me, that took the place of Larry and what I heard from him. I intentionally stared, waiting for him to enlighten me on the young women in *jeans,* with blonde and slender outlines, some on top, others under the orange trees. All in a light roar, a lively giggle, tossing each other around, collecting the golden fruit, in a contented fuss. I had the feeling they were not people from the kibbutz. We approached. They looked at us as we passed, we exchanged wishes of *boker tov,* of a happy morning. Short moments in which they suspended their work, then they resumed their task. Again, the oranges jumped from hand to hand until they were collected amid calls, exclamations and laughter.

Volunteers who came for a few months; these were Dutch, Larry told me. They learn a few things about agriculture, the basics of Hebrew and, *last but not least,* they experience community life. There was no lack of young Germans either, he told me to my astonishment. Some arrived with the confessed intention of serving, of making up for the crimes of their relatives. Sometimes of their own parents. Strangely enough, it's not uncommon for them to insist on recounting stories of suffering without being asked a question.

As the morning progressed, I discovered a different Larry. I knew him to be military. He had fought in the 1948 war of Israel's independence, not having to wait long before being highly promoted. Between the cypresses and the orange groves, I now saw him as a son of the earth, drawing from time to time a vague deep smile that soon faded. Someone who discreetly fed on veiled forces, telluric energies, those that throbbed and vibrated in him; no, it was no longer the same Larry who sat rocking, mute, between the walls of the house.

"Let's sit down for a while, Alan," Larry told me, as we passed an ordinary wooden bench on the path. It was the first time I had ever heard him say my name, which gave me an unexpected and childlike pleasure. We had already passed the orchard, we could see it in its greatness. The sun was high, making the fruits sparkle like little magic lights among the strong and thick green foliage.

Larry cut the silence that had been created in the meantime to tell me: "Today, I'll take you to the rose garden, one of our big investments." But he had barely said it and immediately his gaze was fixed on the figure approaching from afar, to warn me laconically: "look who's coming." He said nothing more. I didn't ask either. With a fresh puff of smoke, he informed me, "You'll be pleased to meet him, Alan."

We stood up and walked toward him. Until I could see who it was. He was an elderly man walking forward at a slow pace, leaning on a cane. He was protected by a cloth panama, round and grey, and by powerful sunglasses that covered a large part of his face. We met. Brief words were exchanged between Larry and the newcomer. But enough for him to unexpectedly turn to me and take my hand and tell me, "It's a great pleasure to meet you. I knew you were coming, but I didn't know the exact date. It's really a great pleasure, believe me. You can't leave without a long conversation; when can you come and have tea with me?"

To my astonishment, he had said it in fluent Portuguese, in a happy and singing tone, denoting the breath of other breezes. He did so, his hand already on my shoulder, waiting for my reaction.

"If you want, this afternoon," Larry suggested.

Hence, not having any idea about the person I was to meet, I agreed and arranged with him that same day I would visit him at his house at five o'clock in the afternoon. Larry would take me there.

The stranger said goodbye to me with a light tap on the shoulder, and then said, "I'll be waiting for you, it will be a great pleasure to talk to you."

When we were alone, Larry summed it up by saying that he was a well-known jurist, a law professor, an interesting person.

Then the two of us proceeded along unmade paths, until we came to a very extensive greenhouse. The rose garden.

Larry decided to put out the pipe he smoked, and immediately a discreet smile opened up that was no longer unknown to me. We entered, with the respect of someone entering a temple, and found ourselves facing a vast space where Larry cultivated *his* roses. Yellow, purple, lilac, white, some climbing, others almost dwarf, roses with a plump corolla or a soberer crown, all of them surrounded at his feet by thin rubber tubes assuring the irrigation. Ambience of a tepid serenity. Then Larry told me the story of the rose garden, created on his initiative, without neglecting to point out that since his youth in Vienna, the study and cultivation of roses had been one of his favourite *hobbies*. It was not easy to convince the kibbutz members that this was a good investment to make, but after many repeated debates they finally agreed. At first, experimentally, on a small scale, then we would see. However, it wasn't long before the people of the kibbutz recognised that this was indeed a venture to be undertaken. Soon after, Larry was already making it rain before me strange numbers, but the most significant ones seemed to concern the export figures and dates, many of which coincided with the European end-of-year festivities. Meanwhile, he crouched down, and so did I, in order to give me a detailed explanation of the irrigation system through thin and dark pipes that I had seen, considered as an important innovation of the country in the agricultural sector. All this he said in an almost excitement that I had met him shortly before, so I had to recognise that had it not been for that walk through the fields, I would have been left ignorant of how much of the inner life of that devoted pioneer and soldier.

However, the truth is that my thoughts were racing away, wanting to make hours jump. Ah, if only I could, in those moments, move the hands forward, anxious that five o'clock would come! Larry must have picked up one or two impatient signals from me, so the visit to the rose garden was not as detailed as he had wanted. And I didn't regret it, because it had already become clear to me that the *modus vivendi of* the kibbutz allowed the free expression of feelings and emotions. There was a new and grateful stamp of authenticity in the web of relationships between everyone. I also just had the opportunity not to hide what was inside me.

Five o'clock. Professor Rosenberg's house. Larry drove me there. I saw myself alone at the door. Ground floor house clad in strips of bluish wood, similar to the one I had been given. A window, in front a lawn deserving greater care. I knocked lightly on the door, which opened almost immediately. I was greeted by eyes of a brilliant blue, denoting joy. A lot of white hair, a slight curvature of the spine that nevertheless did not let him look small. In his late seventies. I entered. The space was short, and even smaller given the shelves full of books that lined the walls from floor to ceiling. A round table, wooden armchairs cushioned all around. We sat down. A tepid stillness reigned, an ancient sobriety.

I let myself be taken by unexpected calmness. My host waited with a discreet smile, still guessing me a certain embarrassment. Then he asked. First, he wanted to know details about my family's relationship with Gretel; he inquired about my mother and how she arrived in Portugal, then about our community and Jewish life. Following, he interrogated about my studies and the university where I did them and finally about the reason that brought me to Israel. It became clear to me that Professor Rosenberg would not miss a word of what I told him. Moreover, in the promptness, the rigor of his words, even in his way of listening, he let me understand an ingrained habit of reflection, the taste and cult of analysis, a deep-rooted *sagesse*. At least that is how I understood it.

At a certain moment, it was my turn to ask, and the question immediately arose as to how my interlocutor had obtained that fluent and elegant Portuguese of which he had immediately given me proof. Professor Rosenberg then told me.

Measuring, weighing the words, he spread himself a little. He had taught law at the University of Vienna, from where his colleagues had expelled him in the 1930s. He said this with the naturalness of one who bears no grudge, reconciled with misfortune. The law faculty of the Hebrew University in Jerusalem, where he had taught generations of jurists, would become his true home. Personally, he was even grateful for the opportunities that life had offered him.

"And Portuguese, Professor, how did you learn it?" I asked.

"I have not forgotten your question and I will answer it in a moment, but first allow me to prepare you some hot tea. We've had some cold days. This is one of them."

A little while later, he was telling me, "You should know that I was also in Portugal. This is a long story, but I will not tire you by going into details. I must already tell you that you come from a country which I esteem and to which I owe a great deal. That is another reason for the great pleasure I take in our meeting."

With brief words, and a frank smile, my host let me

realize how pleasant it was for him to go through the intricacies of a long life, stimulating his memory, filling gaps and that in the company of someone who was willing to listen to him in a language he had not used for a long time, and which he seemed to cherish.

"It was in the time of Professor Salazar," he continued. "How long he has lasted, that ruler! I tell you that it was a great privilege to have been in Portugal. You will certainly be aware of the many Jews who arrived there, some who settled there, others who left. Lisbon played a very important role at that time, also on the humanitarian side, as you are well aware. As I said to you, I have also been in Portugal and the experience I had was very gratifying."

Professor Rosenberg got up, went to the *kitchenette*, from where he returned with a steaming teapot. He filled my cup, then sat down.

"But why Portugal, what took you there, Professor?" I enquired.

"Since you are interested, I will tell you in some detail how things happened. I am very grateful to you for your patience in listening. At the time of the *Anschluss*, my main objective was to go to Palestine. This required an entry visa, which was not at all easy because of the restrictive British policy. I'm sure you know what happened. So, I thought, maybe a solution would be for me to come to Portugal, known for its old and, let's say, friendly relations with the British. Perhaps then, who knows, I would have the possibility of obtaining the desired visa. But things did not turn out as I had planned. You will soon find out why. The fact is that I managed to leave Austria just in time on a train full of refugees. I will not tell you how it went, but only the end of events. We travelled through Spain on a train with windows completely shut, in absolute darkness. Until we crossed the border. There, upon arrival in your country, things soon began to change. The Portuguese government came to organise reception centres for the newly arrived immigrants. During this time, the authorities and also the population showed great humanity and a very spontaneous courtesy. I will explain to you why. I came to live in a small and beautiful city not far from the capital – yes, yes, you are right, that was the name, Caldas... the Caldas da Rainha. The population was very affectionate, very welcoming. I can tell you that even the judge, the prosecutor and some local lawyers came to greet me at the retreat centre, after they heard that a law professor from the University of Vienna was there. Look at that! We who had been so badly treated in our homeland and how we came to be received! And then, you know, we had beautiful conversations. Everybody was aware of the theories developed by great Austrian Jewish jurists like Jellinek and Hans Kelsen, and they were especially very surprised and curious when they heard about the meetings that Kelsen, my colleague, and I had with Sigmund Freud. What good people I came to meet in your country. What a beautiful country you have!"

"But as for your Portuguese, Professor – and I hope I don't bother you with my insistence – how did you achieve such fluency?"

"You see, my young friend, in Portugal I met a Brazilian lady, so my destiny was no longer Palestine but Brazil. There, believe me, after a while I became a farmer in the wilderness, '*ao Deus dará*' (God will give it) and that for half a dozen years. Then I studied Portuguese, which is so rich. You will excuse me, sir, but just now I used the expression '*Deus dará*' that I have not used for many, many years. In Brazil, they say it originated in Recife, in the seventeenth century. There are those who argue that it is linked to the story of a merchant who, when he was unable to stock up on merchandise, apologised by saying, '*Deus dará*'. So much so that his surname became Deus dará and was transmitted to his descendants. Curiosities of a language that is not at all easy, and above all very interesting. But still answering your question, during that time in Brazil I fell in love with the writing of Ferreira de Castro and Aquilino. What great writers! As I was telling you – and excuse this interruption – my time in Brazil was limited, since my wife and I decided to come to Israel. Here, I taught for about twenty years."

Professor Rosenberg rose to pour me some more tea.

"It was after my wife passed away that our daughter Tali insisted that I come to live near her on the kibbutz. Here you see me, my dear sir. But it has been a very enjoyable time for me. Your cousins are charming people. Larry, a vice-general in the reserve, is the great mover of the kibbutz. Did you know that he was an excellent poet who in his Vienna days was already beginning to be known as such? And of your cousin Gretel, what can I tell you? A brave woman! Tell me, sir, how is your country doing?"

I told him about the colonial war; about a university that was not, as it should be, lacking academic freedom; of the student crisis; of living proudly alone; of a country that has become a champion of lost causes; of a growing claustrophobia...

Professor Rosenberg took advantage of my pause to take up a theme common to our two countries.

"Lamentable, these endless wars. Also the beautiful Portugal involved in a complicated conflict. Professor Salazar will have had the merit of not letting the country get involved in the last war, it is a pity that he is not recognising that the destiny of the colonies is one, their independence. But let me tell you, our situation is also very complex, and more so it could become if we do not manage to disengage quickly from the territories now occupied. And I fear very much that our politicians are not understanding the harm that could come from this latest military victory… But I will not trouble you with this matter of the possible repercussions of the Six-Day War. Changing the subject, you will allow me a question: would you like to come and continue your studies, perhaps do a PhD, among us? Know that we have in our faculty a new generation of excellent professors on whom you can rely. Think about it. Don't forget."

It was not long before I asked permission to leave. Professor Rosenberg's downcast gaze had begun to reveal that natural fatigue of one who touches up in the crusted crevices of memory. Short silence. Suddenly, he stared at me again to tell me, with a hint of diffidence, "I've never been back to your country, so I have a request to make of you; if one day you have the opportunity to pass through that beautiful city, Caldas, take some photographs and send them to me. If I'm not mistaken, it was there that a great artist also lived, by the name of… Bordalo, yes, yes, that's it, Bordalo Pinheiro; and there was the fruit market and a very nice café, opposite, all very nice…"

Then it was Rosenberg's turn to slowly, cautiously stand up and thank me for the visit.

After we parted, he waited static by the door until I

walked away.

In my room. I lit the dim and naked lamp. I threw myself on the bed. From there, I quickly reviewed the modest cubicle where I was. Suddenly, a serene joy touched me, the kind that only simple things, humble and unpretentious people can awaken. My cousins. I saw them in their simplicity, in the cheerfulness with which they had been able to turn their lives around after such dark nights. For the moment, Larry, who in Professor Rosenberg's words could have been a poet of renown, turned reluctant soldier, finally unveiled land worker. And Professor Rosenberg, how naturally he had received me, how frankly he had told me about himself, his misfortunes, taking care to hide his academic career, certainly brave until the moment he joined the people of the kibbutz. The orange grove, the rose bushes, Gretel's tender and distant smile. A whole scene vibrating with ardour, nerve and colour, so far from the grey and cloudy of my country. With sadness, I saw it again. There, I thought I saw a funereal ballet on points where swirled hordes of hollow and vain excellencies, plus a court of dignitaries, meritorious, venerable, magnificent. In a circle, all around, among bowing and trembling was the caper of an inexhaustible doctoral crowd flaunting titles, some more inflated and extensive, so many in a joint posture of kissing and rapprochement to see who could best fulfil and pamper. The people, summed up in a single smirk, valiant and suffering, sitting in the background humming an old *faduncho* and spinning little balls from a rosary in their hands. This was so as long as it was ordered by the baton of an old man of eremitic life who wanted everyone under his restrained and provincial dimension, oblivious to the directions of the world, awkward even to understand them.

There was, of course, the promise of young and rebellious minds trying to raise their voices. Such was the grim stage of a medieval and decrepit university, where free thinking had become a sin, sometimes a mortal one, if the duty of piously spewing out mouldy wisdom were violated. But beware, beware, that to ruin the efforts of these daring people there was the omnipresent *pidesco* army, alert and camouflaged, informing, informing, taking them with them.

Then I was assailed by Professor Rosenberg's words: *wouldn't you like to come, to continue your studies, why not a doctorate, we have with us a new generation of great teachers, think about it*. His glare did not leave me, in the midst of a sea of doubts, indecisions, which had awakened in me and that I was going to have to face. It had left me wrapped in a mixture of balm and adrenaline.

Without warning, suddenly, a new window of opportunity seemed to open up for me. Pure plot? Voices of destiny? Fantastical daydreams?

I saw Gretel, who threw me her downcast look and suffering smile, wanting to calm me down.

Perplexity of me.

Still in the room, it was Carole who came to my aid. I remembered her. She looked at me with her laughing face that was as submissive as it was domineering. I had met her shortly before, in Tel Aviv, in the hotel where I had stayed for a few days. This was an inn without any stars, of the family type, where the owner was the one who received and registered the guests, served breakfast early in the morning, while joking with each one without expecting any reply. With that ease that only the master of the house knows how to have.

On the very first day, he told me, "Nice morning, *boker tov*. Listen, I made your coffee at the end table with the young lady over there. See her? She came alone, sit with her, keep her company. Then take her for a walk, it's always better for both of you if you're accompanied."

He said it with the singleness of one who does a good deed. But then the practical sense. "That'll save me a table too."

I respected my innkeeper's wishes. That's how I met Carole. Coming from Paris. As she sipped a juice, out of the corner escaped her the gaze of an obstinate blue. Once, twice, then a restrained smile could already be glimpsed. It didn't last long until the dialogue sprang up with the naturalness of things that wait for the moment to be said.

No, she was not happy to be in Israel. It was her parents who wouldn't leave her alone, always insisting that she come. Now she was waiting for some uncles from her mother's side who lived in Beersheva, and with whom she would stay for a season. No, of course she wouldn't trade Paris for anything, much less a small town on the edge of the desert.

As we were leaving, the owner of the little hotel – luckily situated in an alley in the city centre – had still told us, "Distract yourselves, *teenu*."

We strolled around the vicinity, along the avenues Keren Kayemet and Nordau, along Arlosorof, then continued until almost by the sea. It was then that Carole came out with her bleak comments.

"And they say this is the main avenue of Tel Aviv! Look at all this poor housing, the shops stuck together! *Quel horreur!* And if this is Televive, how can the rest be different? All done in a hurry, and with such a lack of taste!"

I let her speak. I was interested in listening to her, without interfering, I felt the frankness of her words.

She continued, "Still such a crude country, don't you think? The airport, what poverty, facilities that look more like those of a provincial warehouse. The ceilings are covered with half-varnished bamboo, who would have thought it! Is this how a country that wants to dictate the rules presents itself right from the start?"

My words, in an attempt to convince her that Israel had other priorities, especially those touching on its own defence and integration of the *olim* arriving from everywhere, would not have touched her eardrums. I let Carole continue.

"Two days ago, imagine, I went for a bus ride to get an idea of the city, the people, the shops, in short, how to live. No sooner had a moment passed than the person sitting next to me started a you, you, you and you with me, as if I was obliged to answer. Where are you from? Oh, Paris *est-ce- que tu viens de faire ton aliah? Non, alors qu'est-ce-que tu attends? Et tes parents d'où sont-ils? Tu est venue toute seule?* And if the person gets entangled and doesn't stop the conversation, the questionnaire goes on and on, as if it were absolutely natural to get intimate with the first stranger who sits down next to us. Or do they think that having taken the same bus at the same time is enough to create a familiar relationship? *Quelle petitesse!*"

A new initiative of mine to clarify that the great feeling of loneliness that reigned in Israel would be counterbalanced by these and other manifestations of solidarity with the Jews who were arriving would have produced in Carole the effect of a dragonfly passing her by. Nothing could be done. She definitely hated the style.

On a terrace. The Mediterranean stretching out, low, like an embroidered tapestry that rolls up, unrolls and spreads without noise. A grey, lethargic sky. Birds in whimsical sinuosities at the water's edge. Carole. I saw her profile, her slender, haughty neck like a swan emerging from a thick sweater, then her plump lips that turned in defiance. A grey wool cap from which her long, blonde hair fell. From time to time, she shot me an oblique glance, a gentle blue ray. The sand that awaited us. Hands that sought each other. Then she ran away from me, ran like a happy child, waiting for me to grab her. We rolled in the sand. The sea almost touched us.

"*Et à Paris, tu te sens bien là-bas?*"

"*Pas toujours. Tu sais, mes copains à l'université ils sont tellement snobs, à sa manière. Tu dois lire tous les Pauls, le Paul-Jean Toulet, Paul Claudel, Paul Valéry, Paul Éluard. Ah, bon, et Jean-Paul Sartre, tout le Sartre, bien sûr. Et les discussions sans fin, les comparaisons, quel est le meilleur, si Mallarmé, Verlaine ou Rimbaud, et Camus, le nouveau roman, Robbe-Grillet... Tu ne peux pas manquer une seule lecture, tu vois?*"

Again, I remembered my country and thought how stimulating it must be what I heard. And I told her so. But she soon reacted by making it clear that they were ready to make fun of everything and everyone at the slightest opportunity. And she went on.

"One day when I decided to reread Daudet's *Petit Chose*, and I told them how much the book had moved me, they burst into a laugh. I became *La Petite, La Belle Chose. Et en musique c'est le même. Il faut absolument que tu aimes Brassens, et Ferrat, et Léo Ferré, et tant d'autres, et Collette Magny, et Francesca Solleville, et Henri Tachan. Moi je suis comme je suis faite interdite d'avouer que j'adore Adamo, sa voix calme et sensuelle, surtout quand il chante 'Ma brune', 'Mes mains sur tes hanches', 'Les filles du bord de mer'. Ça m'énerve! Ils me croient tout à fait enfantine. Moi, moi je m'en fous."*

Suddenly, I saw Carole walk away, she followed the beach with her arms up, ran, jumped, then returned, whirling, to tell me, her lips next to mine, *"Je suis comme je suis. Je suis faite comme ça Quand j'ai envie de rire Oui je ris aux éclats J'aime celui qui m'aime."*

Already a little distant, I still heard her.

"Est-ce ma faute à moi Si ce n'est pas le même Que j'aime chaque fois Je suis comme je suis Je suis faite comme ça."

It was already evening when we returned to the hotel. The owner-receptionist-breakfast server was the one who came to open the door. He didn't show any strangeness when he saw us hugging. He said nothing, other than his *laila tov* wishes. I followed Carole to her room. Slowly, she turned the key. The door already ajar. A look that inquires, that challenges, *"Tu viens?"*

Gretel. I anxiously needed to be alone with her. Even in silence. Meanwhile, time was passing. That's why it was with great joy that I heard her say to me in the dining hall, "Alan, tomorrow afternoon I want you at the house."

It was fading day when we sat around a low, round table. Behind Gretel, the large window looking out, through which water caterpillars zig-zagged capriciously.

There were brief moments in which we looked at each other. Gretel took advantage of these moments to spin the record with Nomi Shemer's song "Yerushalaim shel Zaav" [Golden Jerusalem], which celebrated the victory in the Six-Day War in June.

What to say? I would have started by asking her, "Gretel, tell me about yourself. What was it like when you came? What's it been like?"

She must have thought, *It's a pity you're coming so late, Alan, when my time is almost up.* So, we started with vague words, the kind that sometimes break until you find the thread of the conversation.

It was when she stood up to pour me tea that I saw her irrepressible grimace, her torso bent under unrestrained pain.

"Gretel, why?"

"Let's just talk about what it was, Alan. I'm fine. I don't want to ruin any of your time with us."

As a child, I used to think that my mother's family never really existed. I had only known them through black and white photos, some already faded. Sometimes, they were of people in groups, whom my mother said were uncles, cousins, many staring at us with a serious look. So, I was sure I had a large family, which was therefore nothing more than a reasonable ream of photographs. So it was that one day I met Gretel, a little girl, hugging my mother. And I told her.

Gretel looked at me closely, but her gaze did not penetrate deeply. I felt her veiled sorrow. Nomi Shemer's voice took over and we listened to her almost mystical song about the Jerusalem of gold. Gretel would have felt a renewed breath.

"We still made it, Larry and I. And my sister Ruth, who as I've already told you ended up in Prague, where she still lives. Your mother and I were very close, and similar. They thought of us as sisters. Her dream was to be a doctor; mine, to continue piano studies. Larry never thought he would become a military man, his world was books, writing, writing. It was life that shaped us, Alan, we didn't have the chance to create it and enjoy it to our liking. Anyway, others will come along to fill in what we couldn't accomplish."

I saw her downcast look. Her voice was silent. The hands that spoke with palms turned towards me, as my mother used to do. Then she resumed, a little excited.

"We did everything to survive, Alan. And to regain our dignity, which no one knew how to respect. That was one of the heaviest tasks we had to face, that of regaining esteem for the person we were. Arriving from that wretched Europe, our young people didn't even have time to receive any kind of military instruction. We just disembarked and took up arms to defend ourselves. So it was with Larry and even myself, on the kibbutz. Me too, gun in hand, when all I wanted to do was sit at my piano. Our generation will soon be extinct. We can only dream that our children will enjoy a better future. It is to them that we owe our great debt."

Gretel got up to open a drawer, from which she took out something.

"Oh, I almost forgot, I have here to offer you a picture of the three of us, Larry and I, with Ronit. And also take my ballpoint pen, I have coupons, I can pick up another one. Sorry for the smallness, but as you know everything here in the kibbutz is counted, there is nothing extra. And money to buy outside is something we don't have."

While I listened to her, I saw in Gretel the hard image of a past that was also mine. I rediscovered myself, I situated myself better in time. It became painful to remember the gaps in history; the truncated continuity, with difficulty, resurfaced. The astonishment of myself, fruit of the disproportionate affliction that others went through. Without it, I would not be. Child of injustice and barbarism, I felt repulsed even by myself. The remembrance of a raw truth had availed me the deception of a freedom that one never had, of which we only reap brief and deceptive mirages. And also the pragmatic conviction that in spite of all that happened, no, it was not in the kibbutz that misfortune had prevailed.

The door was opened. Larry came in, shaking himself out of the wet. He said two or three short words to Gretel, then Gretel replied, "Don't worry, I'm happy."

Then, he left us. But before he did, Larry still told me to be ready the next day, early morning. We were going to leave.

At night, in my room. I lay awake. My gaze flitting from one side to the other, in the light of the ceiling, traversing walls, touching the cupboard, again around the lighted lamp, like a dazzled fly. Until it settled on the simple bedside table. There was a drawer. I pulled it out. Inside was the *Torah*. I let it open by itself. The *Parasha Vaierah* of *Genesis* appeared to me. I immersed in it.

"And the Eternal said, 'The cry of Sodom and Gomorrah has increased, and their sin has become very great. I will go down therefore, and see, if they have done as the cry (of the city) which is come unto me, I will make an end of them, and if not, I will know it.' And the men turned from thence, and went to Sodom, and Abraham was yet before the Eternal. And Abraham came near, and said, wilt thou also destroy the righteous with the wicked? There may be fifty righteous ones within the city. Wilt thou also destroy and not forgive the

place for the fifty righteous within it? Far be it from you to do such a thing, to kill the righteous with the wicked; and the righteous shall be equal to the wicked; far be it from you! He that is judge of all the earth, shall he not do justice? And the Eternal said. If I find in Sodom fifty righteous persons within the city, I will pardon the whole place because of them. And Abraham answered and said, Here it is, I began to speak to the Lord, and I am dust and ashes. Of the righteous fifty, five may be missing: wilt thou destroy all the city for the five? And he said, I will not destroy, if I find there forty and five. And he spoke again unto him, and said, Forty peradventure may be found there. And he said, I will not do it because of the forty. And he said, Be not troubled, I pray, O LORD, and I will speak: Thirty peradventure may be found there. And he said, I will not do it, if thirty be found there. And he said, I have taken liberty to speak unto the LORD, perhaps twenty shall be found there. And he said, I will not destroy by twenty. And he said, Be not annoyed, I pray, O LORD, and I will speak only this once: Peradventure ten may be found there. And he said, I will not destroy by the ten. And the Eternal One went away, as soon as he had finished speaking to Abraham, and Abraham returned to his place."

Suddenly, a knock at the door, then another one immediately, and without even having time to ask who or why, I saw Larry rushing into the room, anxious, in a posture that was entirely new to me. "Hurry, Alan, get dressed and run, they're calling us to the dining-room" was all I heard him say.

Everyone was already gathered there, without knowing the reason of the call, and without anyone revealing the will to ask, when suddenly an enormous hand began to reach over the multiple heads (curiously, ignoring mine), passing from one to another, and shouting increasing numbers that the secretary of the kibbutz diligently registered. Until it was Comrade Vilnay who stood up, arms raised in a gesture of victory to loudly announce, "Comrades, we are saved, we have reached the required number, we are, we are…"

Then, with my eyes still on Vilnay preaching numbers, and seeing the people in the refectory dispersing, I got up unsteadily to put out the lamp that had been lit when I fell asleep.

There is always a path that is the last. Sometimes, it takes time for us to understand that it was so. At other times, it is the hidden truth that is not contained, issuing its warnings of what will be. A few weeks later, it was you, Larry, who informed us that Gretel was no more. On a blue sheet of paper, just like the one in which you invited me to visit her.

I had insisted that I return from the kibbutz by bus, just as I arrived, but neither Gretel nor Larry agreed to my request. They told me not to overdo it with my care, because it would do Gretel some good to relieve a bit.

The morning had dawned under a sky of washed blue, without the slightest white lint. Larry, with his pipe, was already waiting for us in the *Renault 4* that the kibbutz had given him. He insisted that I sit next to him. Gretel sat in the back with Ronit who had missed school for that purpose. We were to go on to Jerusalem. All quiet, each one back in their own little world. But in mine, Gretel was the sole inhabitant, for I suspected I would never see her again. As if her last stage had to be so to profoundly alter my life course. She, Gretel, before whom I had known almost nothing. Then I recalled the steps I had to take with the consular services until I discovered her whereabouts. The joy of a first certainty, the indication of a simple address; soon, a short letter that followed, another back calling. That was all.

The road was narrow and poorly finished, and every unevenness of the pavement announced to me the suffering of my cousin. But we both settled into a consensual lie; Gretel in the resigned smile she addressed to me, me in the apparent detachment from her silent pain.

It was Larry who ended the silence to inform us that we were going to cross part of the recently occupied Arab territories. But first, he insisted on taking me to Megiddo. It didn't take long before we got there. There, Ronit and Gretel stayed in the car while Larry and I set off on foot along the bumpy roads, with thousands of stones piled on top of each other. Unexpectedly, a partly unknown side of Larry revealed itself to me. No longer the one who took care of the land, the rose bushes and the orange groves, no longer the poet and pioneer of the kibbutz, but another one, the military man, the curious history buff who told me about the past and the strategic position of Megiddo.

Considered to be one of the oldest inhabited centres in the Middle East, whose origins date back to the seventh millennium before the Christian era, so he said, the stones of Megiddo bring together traces of more than twenty overlapping cities. Mentioned in ancient Egyptian writings, Megiddo is also referred to in the Bible as Derech Hayam, a name which the Romans literally translated as Via Maris. Larry went on to point out the importance of Megiddo to the time of King Solomon, for it was there that he gathered many of his triumphal chariots, the traces of the multiple chariot stables still being quite visible. Interestingly, given the large number of battles fought at Megiddo and mentioned in the Bible, the name Megiddo itself acquired a warlike meaning. More recently – Larry told me – General Allenby had also been there during the British invasion of Palestine in the First World War. Hence the title Lord Allenby of Megiddo. Larry explained to me all this as we stumbled over an unspeakable number of piled-up stones. Then, with less effort, he referred to the theological reason that justified the celebrity of the place.

"According to Christian eschatology, that would be the site of Armageddon, the one where the final battle will take place – the ultimate battle between the forces of light and darkness, good and evil. It will be there that Christ and the Antichrist will have to face each other. Also, Megiddo gives you a glimpse, Alan, of the vast archaeological world we have to reveal. Archaeology will come to prove much of what the Bible tells us, let's hope it becomes a real challenge, almost a national sport."

Shortly afterwards, we collected to the car. Ronit greeted us with a short, angry growl of impatience.

We followed a narrow and patched road cutting through parched and stony land, here and there, flanked by a spontaneous and low grove of trees, spaced eucalyptus, a world where one would say no man's hand had entered. We passed Jenin, then Shehem, and the impression had been about the same: a chaotic scene of intersecting cars and carts, among modest sand-coloured buildings, protesting honks, men in *keffiya*, women with their heads covered with their *hijab*, others with their faces sealed by the *niqab*, but also young men in *jeans* running riot from one side to the other. In between were groups of young-looking soldiers in their green suits. However, one could not conclude that the Israeli presence had substantially altered the flow of daily life in these occupied lands. Hence, it occurred to me to wonder what would have happened if the outcome of the war had been different and Nasser had achieved his objective, which was to throw the Jews into the sea. Certainly carnage.

But to break the silence, I still asked Larry what we could expect if we had a breakdown there. The answer came fast and short. "Don't open the devil's mouth…"

Shortly thereafter, Ramalah, with its loud, noisy, disjointed traffic, bringing us the same sense of strange land we've previously picked up. As we waited for the green light of the traffic, it was Larry's turn to open up a little more. He said to me, "We've got a hot chestnut on our hands, Alan. Military victory does not mean we have obtained peace. On the contrary, if we do not seize the opportunity to negotiate, handing back the territories in exchange for unconditional recognition of Israel by the Arab world, we will have created the conditions for other and other wars will follow. And each one will be more difficult than the last. But even if this is not so," he concluded, "I don't see that we have the material means, nor the moral reasons to control the daily life of a population that doesn't want us."

Behind, Ronit mumbled again and again sighed, wails of boredom. Tired of our conversation. The time had come for Larry to pay attention to her. So there followed, from time to time, mini-dialogues between the two of them, which systematically ended with a well-known Ronit *lô*. What had Larry asked or suggested? Some detour on the route, a hypothetical stop, a visit to some historical site within walking distance? Whatever it was, one thing was certain: the father, the military man, the quasi-general was under the command of that whimsical child with piercing, hurtful brown eyes.

Meanwhile, I took the opportunity to unexpectedly turn to Gretel. I saw her gaze clenched in a grimace of deep, mute pain.

I longed to get to Jerusalem, where I would stay for two or three days. However, more than the excitement of the visit – the Old City, the Wailing Wall, Yad Vashem, the temples of Omar and Aksa, the Holy Sepulchre and so many other places – I felt remorse for seeing those three making the return journey. The embarrassment was certainly greater, given Gretel's perilous condition.

Until we arrived in Jerusalem. We headed straight to the YMCA, a short distance from the Old City, where luckily Larry had arranged for me to stay.

The moment of farewell. A whirlwind of feelings in which the best and most eloquent is silent speech. And so it was. We embraced in silence. Gretel smiled. I was already out of the car, without the car moving. Larry would have asked Ronit if it was time to leave, to which she would have retorted with her peremptory *lô*. I turned around. Ronit's face, toward me, glued to the glass of the door. I approached and the two of us stared at each other, face to face. This had been the first and only time we had ever faced each other. Down Ronit's tawny face, slowly two sinuous tears trickled down.

I drove away. The car followed.

III

That's How I Met You, Dana

I only had two days left before I returned to my small court in the South, with many inquiries to be made. And I needed that time. But this time, I would be the one being questioned, and there was no lack of questions being asked with disturbing insistence. When something like that happened, I would get into my Beetle and let myself go. That day, she decided to go to the waterfront. She knew well how enchanted I was by that tongue of a road, first around the river, then facing the sea, bordered by houses, some palatial, others small and provincial, all in a soft and quiet intimacy, noble and plebeian. Road where there are death curves, forts to defend the coast, some taller, others a little more frightened, toy boats that here and there swing on beach shells, it is the waterfront of childhood, of Sunday afternoons, and not only, where the black ministerial Mercedes with closed curtains strutted, the *MG* convertibles with their infallible blonde hair blowing in the wind, but also the plebeian carts with the head of the family entertaining the kids, that's where my Beetle took me, rumbling.

After wandering a bit through the alleys of Cascais, she stopped and waited for me to leave. We were at the Albatroz; the doubt had still arisen between leaving me there or continuing on to the dunes of the Guincho, but we agreed that we preferred the gentleness of the bay under the squeals of the seagulls to the sandy gale of a rough sea.

Already comfortably seated. Luckily, no one was around. All I needed was the double *Gordon*, which soon arrived in a joyful effervescence.

Each one will certainly have their enchanted well (it was the Petit Prince who said it, *ce qui embellit le désert, c'est qu'il cache un puits quelque part...*), their blue grotto, and again and again the attraction of the abyss, the urgency of recollection forces us to take a look. As to the depth to which one descends in this practice of personal *diving*, this is a question that goes beyond the modesty of these lines. In other words, it is a matter of spying on our hidden and obscure corners, and it is up to each one to find the best way to proceed. It is often necessary to obtain some support and encouragement. For the moment, the double *Gordon* would suffice for me.

I confess that I did not need to go very deep. A certain and diaphanous truth came to me. It was clear to me that, whatever I wanted, it was not going to be easy to return to the old provincial court. I would probably have to give up, change course.

The João Cipriano case came to my mind, the most urgent. The case was waiting for me, after the investigation phase. Therefore, in articles of necessarily provisional plea, I had to accuse João Cipriano because, at dusk, some day of November nineteen hundred and sixty-something, he had jumped over the border. Since João Cipriano, the father of a litter of five puppies, had not found anyone to provide him with the means to support them, so João Cipriano had to find someone who needed him and paid for his service. But because he had done so without the necessary paperwork with seal and stamp – which added to the bad luck of the guard coming to find him, although some luck was worth it, because it was not necessary to shoot since the fugitive soon gave himself up – it was now up to me, by duty of office and for the good of the nation, to accuse João Cipriano, and after the decision of His Honour, to keep him in a closed jail, which for this purpose, the fact that he had some hungry kids at home was quite irrelevant.

Just me, newly arrived from a country made of refugees, charged with caging João Cipriano and so many others to his measure, then, made charitable, visiting them in the dungeon as a Good Samaritan, no, that was not for me, something would have to change.

"*Psst*," I called the waiter, "I want another double." But he doesn't give me a damn, he turns his back and stays there.

Then, coming towards me, whirling around me, came Gretel and Larry and what I had heard to them, plus the little houses of the kibbutz and the glowing orange groves, the solidary dining hall and even the lecture I had not heard from Comrade Vilnay. Also, Professor Rosenberg in the quiet of a house lined with books, with his insistence: *wouldn't you like to come, to continue your studies here?* A whole nation being assembled stone by stone, different lesson of life, while there, a short distance away, in a private fort facing the sea, an old man turned autistic was busy contemplating the liners crammed with soldiers, on course for... in defence of... that should be so, who knows why. And the PIDE, the PIDE, spying everywhere, through every crack in the door and keyhole, probably even knew I'd had a double *gin*. "*Psst*", I called the waiter again, whom I wanted to ask for another double, but he showed me his side again, and in this, when I was already out of the blue well with my irreducible and insofismable truth, it was then that, suddenly, "Oh man, you've been here!" It was Diogo, a colleague from college, it was a good thing the bloody waiter wouldn't listen to me, if I'd had another double, it wouldn't have been easy for me to simulate smiles and parrot trifles as is usual in such circumstances.

"Meet my girlfriend, Clô, and a friend..." (He said the name, I didn't get it).

By the way, the young girl that accompanied them was a sweet face with a soft olive green gaze. Later, when I said that I had arrived two days before, Diogo took the opportunity to clarify that he frequently went to Cairo, where his father had business. He never went to Tel Aviv but the day would come when he would go there; meanwhile, she, the girl with the soft olive green eyes, wouldn't let go of me. She didn't seem to miss a word, as if I still had some old stuff from other parts attached to me, because she studied history, but what she liked was archaeology.

"The problem is that, as you know," she told me, "archaeology in our country is in the doldrums, a real disgrace, so I'm going to be interested in talking with you. By the way, I recently read some books by Werner Keller..." That's what I heard. When saying goodbye, she also said, "Diogo, take down the phone number of your friend... Alan, yes, sorry, Alan, we are going to have a party in my house in a few days..." That's what I think I understood. "I would really like you to come." I promised.

We talked afterwards about I don't know what, I don't remember, I think it was Diogo telling stories about the summer in Corsica, or if not Corsica, then Malta, or maybe Sardinia, because he had fun making us jump from port to port. Clô, holding his hand, wouldn't stop staring at him, and as she laughed a lot at Diogo's jokes, she gave a sign that they were funny, so we all laughed, until they finished drinking some juices. I was told not to forget to come to the party, and I promised once again. They left.

    That's how I met you, Dana.

IV

Coming Back

Return. No small amount of strangeness. The dubious feeling of not being where I had arrived and, perhaps, of not wanting the destination that awaited me. But I had to. Travels had always caused me an unspeakable maladjustment, a singular ambiguity, but now it was more than that. Broken in two. Nowhere. Not even Paris, where I had stopped for two days, had helped me, with the trampling of the *boulevards*, the bustle of the *magasins*. I had still searched the Garnier-Flammarion to see if I could find a work by Maupassant that I had not read, but the search was not as passionate as it had been in the past. Something was happening. It was worth an afternoon hearing the Madeleine organ and a hurried tour of the Quartier Latin. And I, who loved Paris, found myself there, wandering in conversation with Gretel; also through the orange groves with Larry, repeating to me the paradoxically happy story of Professor Rosenberg; reviewing Ronit's terminating *lô,* her round, tear-brown gaze at parting. And so much else in apparent disorder.

Now it's my Beetle, the HI-43-24, that would take me and accelerate hard. Towards the South. As always on these journeys, in a frantic rush, often jumping over unexpected patches in the road, I hoped this time I wouldn't come across an unwary bird smashing against the front window. I had to get there, and fast.

Next day, close to eight in the morning. In the sixties. Sitting in Moreno's coffee shop, with a bread roll and a coffee. Minutes from the courthouse. At this, "Sir! Are you here yet? Hi, hi, hi!" It was Esteves, the head of Secretariat, approaching, all petty. He had his hair done, with a wink of an eye, and his melon-like head resting on a short rectangle of a nourished body. A sinker. Or as a former colleague would say, referring to one of the professors, a half-wit, five kings of people. And the perfect line of teeth, as if made to measure, plus the thick triangle of the tie giving itself airs.

Then Esteves on the attack. "Does the *sotôr* know about the Pim-Pam-Pum scandal? Oh, doesn't he? Because in the village they don't talk about anything else. It was Moreno who found out. Hi, hi, hi! He's the one who found out about the mariola. And does the *sotôr* know who the cat was? No less than Pais, yes, Pais, the stagecoach officer. Now you see what the local people aren't saying about the court. Oh, don't you know what Pim-Pam-Pum is? Well, I thought you did. It's the supplement that comes out of the Sunday paper with a lot of charades, football matches, crossword puzzles and other stuff to pass the time. That's right, the *sotôr* had already told me that you have no interest in football and pilgrimages. Hi, hi, hi! But you see what happened, don't you? Moreno, that Maltese guy, was the one who used to put the newspaper there, until he started noticing Pim-Pam-Pum was missing.

"We were even asking, Moreno, what happened to the little newspaper? So what does he decide to do, the rascal? He puts himself behind that column doing gossip, yes, yes, the one at the end, no, the other one further to the left, and he lets himself get away with it to detect who the guy was. And he discovered, *sotôr*, it was Pais, imagine that! And Moreno, who is a good dog, caught Pais, he put him in the street shouting in front of everybody, eh, *valdevino*, eh, *pantaminêro*, don't come here again or I'll beat you on the horns, and Pais disappeared, tail between his legs. Hey, *sotôr*, only seen! Hi, hi, hi! The poor man caught in the act of snitching the Pim-Pam-Pum! Free newspaper, hi, hi! So you arrived tonight, did you have a good trip?"

With the soliloquy over, I left Esteves delighted, reviewing Moreno's espionage skills and speculating on how Pais would get that boot off. I ran out the door and took a deep breath.

Closed in my office. On the desk, files that during my absence were piled up, they were about illegal partridge hunting, fights and drunken brawls, two accidents on the road with minor injuries, the theft of a few poultry, and one, two, three, four, five reports about people who tried to jump over the border. One of them, that of João Cipriano, was the most urgent.

However, despite the effort, the fact is that I could not concentrate. I wasn't up to it. I opened the door and went out.

The narrow corridor, rotten wooden floor and ceiling, walls stained by the sweat of time, large window with cracks where winter creeps in. In the waiting, a row of muted people of an ancient hush, an immobile and mournful stain, I also saw them, thick and bare feet used to tread miles.

At this, the angry voice of a more afflicted father. "If you don't sit quietly, you'll get a beating!" The eyes of the kid went down to the ground. Instead, it's you, Ronit, who appeared to me, I saw your defiant look, I heard your imperative *ló* to the vice-general father, who obeyed you. The two children will be roughly the same age, and the instant question is a why.

I walked out the door of the courthouse. A sharp shiver of wind aroused me, but did not allow for delay. I returned to the office. I rummaged through the files, my attention was short. I insisted that for this I am paid; however, I saw myself passing from one to another without breath. I ran out of breath in front of that mass of papers sewn with string. I told myself that I would achieve nothing on that day of return. I gave myself a defeat. I left for good.

It was freezing cold. Weather wrapped up. In my Beetle. Warmed me up with the dirty heat of the engine. I went around the streets of the village, up and down, up and down, until I took the direction of the mine. In front of me unfolded the polished ribbon of the road. Spaced the olive trees in their secular dormancy. A still eagle flew over me, to tell me that I was not alone.

In the mine. Rough rows of dwellings that belonged to the workers, in a white that had long since turned dirty. Walls that would have heard noisy quarrels, laughter, groans, laments, cries, some singing. I still saw some large houses, sheltered behind a wild grove, belonging to the directors who had left, a glimpse of another life.

"The *sotôr* don't meddle with that! Let them go, don't meddle with it!" Such was the advice of the wise Pimentel, the clerk, in whom I had developed the justified habit of trusting. "When they saw that there was nothing to be gained, they packed their bags and left, and to hell with the workers. Orders to close the case. The *sotôr* won't get anything. Stay out of it!"

It was not the first time that they recommended me to be passive. A short time before, in a case of illegal hunting in the hunting grounds of some noblemen, I had been warned to forget the case, which had been filed by orders from above. The matter was settled, period. "Some ministers were there at the time, *sotôr*, nothing to be done," Pimentel had warned me.

Again, the fresh memory of a country creating its own future. There the urgency of solidarity. The *kibbutz*. Larry, the love of the earth, the perversity of war, the need for peace. Gretel, Professor Rosenberg and the others I had seen in the dining hall, in their shortcuts through the world in the recovery of a shattered dignity. Without pity or truce.

"Nothing to do. Stay out of it. The ministers, *sotôr*, the ministers were there." Advice, warnings permeating my ears, a sad refrain that wouldn't go away. And I couldn't stand those repeated invitations to renounce myself! I had brought with me another lesson that I would not let go. But if it was as I was told, that in the face of illegality and rudeness nothing was to be done, then someone was in a wrong place.

The lagoon. Ducks that at my arrival were startled into an unreasonable clatter. Leaves that rustled with the farewell of the afternoon. In the background, the mountain where the border line became entrenched, invisible, sinister.

Shortly after, back. Anonymous hours. Obscure tones, gypsy breezes. The village spread out on the hill, lit in white. It looked big.

The jail. In the centre of the village. Those passing by don't even notice one or two prisoners with their hands clenched against the bars. They go ahead without paying any attention to them. Only once in a while, on Sunday or on a holy day, does some great soul stop to extend a cigarette or two.

I went there with Francisco, the jailer, who, along with his wife, Cidália, and their son, Janito, lived upstairs. She, a handywoman, was the one who cleaned the cell, prepared and brought down casseroles with some bread-soup, while holding a rope that came out of the house floor. This twice a day.

In prison, a naked lamp, two mattresses, and, of course, a hole where they could squat and relieve themselves. In the meantime, they stayed there waiting for a van to take them to a more serious jail.

There was a day when they began to receive a newspaper every week. There would always be one who could read, for himself and for others. At that time, they would shut up and they heard, but what they wanted to learn about was who had gone to a better world, that the rest didn't count.

Once I sat there with them and learned about the deceased and the masses for the thirtieth day, and the thanks to the charitable souls who wanted to attend them. And since a lot of the news came with pictures, one of them said that among the dead there were even some young people. The little newspaper soon passed from hand to hand so that the pictures could be seen, in a resigned mute.

In short, all there together in a serene whispering with death.

I stuck with the idea that they, inside, and the rest of us, outside, were all equally dead. But it was the dirty and illiterate inmates, whose sole ambition was to find Cidália's steaming casserole dish coming down from the ceiling, who had the best experience and wisdom of what it was like to die day by day.

It was on one of those afternoons, towards the end, that Francisco's voice rushed into my office announcing that one of them had tried to end his life. He couldn't say who had given him the rope, but it was clear that through the bars there was no difficulty at all.

Agostino received us with a look of astonishment at our fright. "Why did you do that, man?" Then he opened his eyes even wider as if expecting us to answer. Two others who were there were silent to say they saw nothing.

We just sat there, Francisco, the prisoners and I, feeding silences. Feeling the softness of the street entering through the bars. Watching when one of them rose to gather the newspapers scattered on the floor with news, crosses and many photographs. Waiting idly, while each one with his crumpled cigarette. Until the lid of the ceiling opened and down came Cidália's smoking pot, plus an old bag. One of the men lifted his dejected body, he and Francisco unfastened the casserole and the cloth to bring inside some pieces of corn bread. Agostino remained static, staring at the rope, wondering if it was the same as the other one he had so clumsily used.

One day. One day, it was said that there was going to be an inspection. Then it seemed that the old walls of the courtroom vibrated with such frenzy, the clerks pacing back and forth in the corridor, carrying reports and more reports, looking circumspect and proficient. This was because the staff, immersed in a self-absorption of months, sometimes years, could not stand any intermission coming from outside. Each one wanting to show, to himself and above all to the others, his high commitment. The motto was that everything should be ready and close at hand.

And even after I made it known that I would be the inspected party, that someone from the capital would come to certify the way I managed the processes, even then the excitement did not subside. There would always be the risk of a badly processed report being due to someone else's fault – imagine the lack of a document, an error in any notification or whatever – and then it would be a problem. It was this, more or less, what they were imagining and fearing. That's why, time and again, there would come the odd question, always from Esteves, who would then pass the information on to the others. "Hey, sir, when are we due?"

At last. A cold morning. Esteves knocked on my door, opened it enough to poke his head in, and with a frown announcing, "Hey, sir, the doctor is already there, hi, hi!"

I went to greet the newcomer outside the courthouse. He took his coat off the car, then put it on with his back to me, took out his briefcase and turned around. I saw his small figure, short forehead, misty eyes, a dull hand shaking hands, all in the manner of a silent film in slow motion.

We were about to enter the courthouse door when I heard him say, "So, right here, next to Spain, huh? One day, we're going to have a serious problem here..." And because I kept silent after such a laconic, but certainly judicious, statement, I would have immediately unleashed a suspicious judgment about myself. He turned back, faced with my negligence. "So, can't you see that at the first opportunity they will want to come in here?"

My astonishment and my obtuseness at such a huge threat caused him a brief and sudden shrug of the shoulders, followed by the oracular truth. "Listen, one day if we lose the overseas provinces, the Spanish will soon attack us! Don't you see the evidence?"

What would I have to add to such a prophecy, so lapidary announced? I admit that the smile that opened up deep inside me gained some visible expression. We had talked. He, an inspector descended from his *turris eburnea*, son of the regime and of order; I, a naïve novice with much to learn. We had barely crossed the courthouse door and I was already sure that I would have to rely on a sworn enemy.

I put my office at his disposal and he stayed there for a few days. I enjoyed the time I spent in the peace and quiet of my house, in Pessoa's company, with one or two visits to the court, in case I had to give some explanation. During those trips, we had brief silent meetings.

When the moment of departure arrived, again the questioning and annoyed voice, "A lot of illegal immigration crime around here, huh? Can you find an explanation for that?"

"So what do you expect, with the misery that goes around here?"

I was pleased to see him quicken his pace a little, settle into the car, make it resound. He took off. I was left with one certainty, I was already catalogued for whatever came and went.

Back to my office. Just then, Esteves carefully opened the door, letting his laughing face glimpse, his caprine voice, "Hey, sir, hasn't the doctor left yet? That was quick, wasn't it? Hi, hi, hi!"

You don't know, Esteves, how many times I've thought about you. I'll tell you why. Because if I had to enlist those I met, happy and content with themselves, I'm sure I wouldn't forget you. One day, you were warned that thinking, giving opinions, is tedious, especially dangerous in those times. Once warned, you knew how to accommodate yourself. Turn your mind around? you may have asked. Let the others do it if they like it. Instead, Esteves, what you were able to create – and you were an expert at it – was a little range of routines, ruses, beliefs, some political, others with a stamp of sanctity, and with such stringent truths you let yourself stay, your curiosity satiated. Then luck also smiled on you, when you pounced on poor Florentina, then you rented a ground floor with two windows to the street, and there you sheltered her, she had the right to go out on Sunday to go to mass, and on other days she should be careful, because you didn't allow a callow woman, and she shouldn't even show herself at the window.

And thanks to your little political devotion, confess it, Esteves, it always earned you a few coins close enough to complete the court's payment, or has it not?

Yes, because they were everywhere, in the courthouse there would have to be someone. I don't have to tell you this evidence. The snitch could only be you. Not Pais, who, as you always proclaimed, was a slob, an idea-crazed, good-for-nothing fool, and who, according to your information, along with your own his! even served as a tail in the villainy.

There was another, an almost errand boy, Ernesto, but he was poor in spirit, an absent-minded man, who could scarcely see the steps ahead.

Until finally, Sunday arrived, Esteves! It was hard to come, but it never missed. Then, after a good night's sleep, it was then that your true hour of *excelsis* would sound. Lord, you would be in Moreno's café, fiercely clutching your steak and sipping the freshly chilled imperial. Serene and tenacious. There was a time when you took Florentina with you; but after one day, you detected a guy looking at her legs, you decided it was better for her to stay quietly at home.

You will wonder how I knew these and other things. It was Moreno, a man who liked booze, who one day, at the top of his drink, sat down at my table. "The *sotôr*, the *sotôr* will excuse me, I've been going round and round, and I have to tell you that it's not only Pais who's a rogue, it's Esteves who's worse, he's scum and only comes here to spy."

I told Moreno that I wouldn't allow him to gossip, but the drunkenness was so strong that he wouldn't let me go. That you, Esteves, only went there to see when the guys started warring and talking about everything, and how life was shit, so that you'd have faith in what had happened. Other times, Moreno said, it was a grind, a nuisance, all mute, and then you wouldn't find a better programme than to pick on him about the hardness of the *bifana*. And there was more Moreno wanted to say, and he only shut up when I gave the matter up and got up to leave. But the little I heard him say was enough to reinforce my suspicions.

You will say that luck has favoured you, and I am sure you will be right. Although as obtuse as an angle, you knew how to live up to your standards, in your small-large world you ruled without rival. Fortunate man that you were, who, as the people say, even the wind gathered his straw. That is why I salute you, Esteves, in your happy king's scarcity.

A couple of weeks later. At home. A wind roared, sweeping the streets. Outside two or three spaced, dying lamps. Grief-stricken windows.

The next morning, there would be trials. One of them was that of João Cipriano, whom I had had to accuse for having wanted to jump over the border. Then I would visit him at the jail, where I was sure someone would be to read the newspaper news about the dead and masses for the thirtieth day. He would wait hungry until Cidália's casserole came down, and for squatting and relief he would rely on the proper hole. As for the cubs, nothing to fear, there would be a generous roof to shelter them.

I briefly opened the large window, and a rushing wind blew and whistled that knew no borders. Just then, the telephone rang. I wondered how many times a day a phone would ring in such a solitary village. This time, it was really mine. I hurried to answer, feeling that at that hour it would be someone friend.

"Diogo!"

"How are you, old boy? Re-adapted already?"

"Doing it for. What about you?"

"Look, next month I have to go to the Middle East, I'll be in your neighbourhood."

"Tel Aviv?"

"No, it's a trip to Cairo. I'm going with Father, who has unfinished business there. I'll tell you about it later. But what brings me here today is another matter, a charge. It was Daniela who asked me to speak to you. Do you remember her? We met in Cascais. She's giving a party at her house next Saturday night; she'd like you to come. Are you free?"

After I promised to go, Diogo also, "You know, Daniela is a nice girl, but a bit shy, she didn't have the nerve to call you, she asked me to do it. As soon as she knows you're

coming, she might call you."
And little else will have been said, other than information about the time and place of the event.

Weekend. Friday afternoon, back to the capital. In my Beetle. I passed fields that I had already seen with the purple strokes of the blueweed, which in times became red with poppies or fresh and jovial with the corn marigold and the tremocils. There were villages of inanimate casitas, cork oaks, olive trees that whisper their melancholy. I looked for the voice of the radio. From it came chants, one after the other. Finally, a very extemporaneous one that recalled the feast, the feast that was a beautiful feast, in which the coming of the king was the most pleasing. Soon the same voice, in a joyful drawl, already ready to greet, whether the king, the queen, or everyone in general. Until a hen rescued me from the torpor into which I had fallen by challenging the wheels of the Beetle, there wrapping itself so as not to leave of itself more than a handful of bloody feathers,
Then I remembered with discreet joy: *Tomorrow night, what will it be like?*

V

Your House, Dana

At the party at your house, Dana, that magic moment when you sought me out. To introduce me to your friends, so you said. But there was more, that your olive-grey eyes would not shut. And so it was that, after a few moments of side-splitting chatter, we danced, our bodies came together, completed each other.

Hidden and brief time, harbinger of some new? Bringing what? Bringing where?

Then, with a scorched memory, it was the return to the old courthouse, to the dragging of afternoons, hours, me recounting the time left until the next meeting, now repeated, of Friday, late afternoon.

That was the time of the Choupana, of Van Gogo, of Palm Beach, the sun gently drowning in the sea of Cascais, while inside sounded the timbre of Tom Jones, the romanticism of Adamo, the Beatles alerting us to when you, me, each one of us reaches *sixty-four*. You, Dana, were singing along with them in a parody tone, unable to imagine us at such a ripe old age.

And I was already hinting that my life might take place somewhere far away…

For those Friday meetings, as you'll remember, I'd pick you up at home. In your square, and while waiting for you in the car, I went back to my childhood days, because I, too, had lived in that same place some time ago. In one of the two or three buildings next to yours. The place remained as it had been, with its old round lake with a loose flow, or emptied and with a pungent aroma due to the uncleaned slime; scattered, green wooden benches where once the maids in uniform would sit and watch over the family's children, whirling on their tricycles; the washed and rosy face of the buildings of the small square in a sleepwalking conversation in which everything had already been said.

Until you arrived. The world faded away. It was you.

But there was a time when you took longer, and then I found myself looking at the building I had lived in. I counted the floors, the windows, I came across the one in the room where one day I stayed to recover from some ailment. It was a warm and grey time during which I became aware of the morning household chores: the opening of the windows, the refreshment of the room; the snorting of the vacuum cleaner; the rattle of pots coming from the kitchen; the freshness of the washed bed. This was the veiled and gentle repose of convalescence.

One morning or another, through the window ajar, the announcement of the florists outside, then the maid who came downstairs, finally the fresh and jovial smell of red carnations brightening the house. Also one or another saleswoman who appeared there at times, her voice hushed, announcing, "Who wants figs?" Or still the haunted and elusive piping of the grinder turning back the clock of time.

You showed up. It's all gone.

It happened that on one of those afternoons you insisted that I go up to your house, no matter how little it was. Also because that time I would have arrived earlier than usual. Although presented naturally, it was clear to me that your suggestion had been previously discussed, even consented to. I accepted. Then I felt your house in a new light, having erased the noisy face with which I had seen it on the day of your party.

The peacefulness of the great room. The carpeted floor where no footsteps could be heard; the mud-green velvet sofas in an invitation to total stillness; the fireplace where a dying fire still glowed; stylish commodes; on the walls, oils, watercolours; on a table a vase of flowers; in the background, in the unusual wait until it was decorated, a little Christmas pine tree.

My eyes ran to some tiny spiky feet that barely touched the ground. Sitting on a little sofa, a so-called *senhorinha*, with flowered fabric, in a corner. The very thin body, almost fleshness, under a shawl of dark embroidery. Coming out of it, the sucked hands walking between themselves in an ancestral cadence the little balls of a rosary. From time to time, the almost imperceptible movement of the lips accompanying that manual and magical turning, in a whisper with the divine. It was your grandmother Marcia, your father's mother, that's what you told me, Dana. Sitting there at the end of the room, not leaving the house unless your mother, or you yourself, took her to the *lausperene*. At my question, you explained to me that it was the name given to the display in churches of a consecrated host, the Blessed Sacrament of the Eucharist, for the adoration of believers. I didn't understand a thing; I just stood there.

Then it was your mother, Camila, who appeared in the room. Tall, light of movement, of a natural elegance. With her, Lilucha, your sister, so cute, clinging to her skirt, acting embarrassed.

Your mother looked at me, it seemed to me, with sympathy. I remember her discreet smile better than the brief conversation we had. At the parting, she pleasantly stressed that when I came to pick you up, I should always come up, instead of staying in the car to wait. Your lowered, biased gaze, Dana, smiled at me. It felt strangely good.

When I returned a week later, the scenario seemed different to me. Not that Grandma Marcia, in her flowery *senhorinha* had interrupted her divine soliloquy for a moment; the difference, Dana, was in your mother. I found her and Lilucha, both sitting on the floor, taking out of some cardboard boxes coloured balls, tiny lamps, bow ties, and other ornaments, while they decorated a dying little pine tree with all those trinkets.

It did not last long before your mother joined us with obvious ease. Soon the conversation sprang up, clean and unadorned.

"So Alan's already started getting his tree fixed? It's always a party, especially if there are children in the house."

"There are no children in my house, and even if there were..."

"So why? Even without children is so beautiful! It's a little joy that you add to the house, you give to the family..."

"You see, a poor pine tree plucked from the earth, no matter how much you adorn it, is meaningless to some."

"Would you care to elaborate, Alan?"

"Mom!"

"In our case, by not keeping the tradition of Christmas."

"So they do not believe in Him, as say, as the Messenger,

the Messiah?"

"Mom!"

"Oh daughter, let us talk, that's how people get along."

"No, I see no reason to celebrate the birth of a man, certainly a good man, a great innovator, who perhaps wanted nothing more than to facilitate compliance with the Law."

"Listen, Alan, one day I'd like to listen to you with more time. We all have our questions, some doubts. You will explain to me the reasons why you do not accept Christ as the true Messiah, the one sent by God. Next time, I'll invite you to stay for dinner. Do you accept? Well, I won't bother you any more for today."

After Camila left the room, in a mixture of agility and coolness, it was Dana's turn to intervene.

"I hope you're not angry, Alan. Mum sometimes likes these kinds of inopportune talks…"

"That's what I appreciated most about her, the spontaneity. She affirmed and asked whatever she felt like without beating around the bush. What's wrong with that?"

"By the way, I'm the one who wants to know. Has your family never had this custom of decorating the house?"

"The truth is they did. My grandfather, poor man, would go out and buy some little pine tree, my mother would dress him up in little balls and bow ties…"

"I can tell by your tone…"

"You're not wrong. At night, I used to get up to dig out a few of those charms and throw them out the window. My mother understood immediately. Christmas was still a long way off, and already the wretched little tree was waiting at the street door for someone who wanted to take it away."

"Alan, you're such a spoilsport…"

"Why lie? Having a pine tree like that travestied in the living room didn't tell us anything. My father didn't even notice. For us, it was a strange habit. Just so our house wouldn't stand out from the others? You know, in my grandparents' time, in Germany, they used to decorate the house with a little fir tree. Then my grandmother would play "Stille Nacht" on the piano, and everyone, bosses and staff sang along, gifts were given, I don't know what more! Tell me, Dana: was it any good? By the way, I'll tell you another one, still related to all this. This time it was about the so-called Santa Claus. My father was sitting with me in the living-room, then the maids came clapping their hands and we all waited. This was because the old man with the white beard was about to arrive with a bag full of presents. Until he came in doing the usual mommies. He came up to me and I asked him, "Where's mother?" Then I accused him, "You are not the Santa Claus, you are the mother!" I pulled his red hat, I pulled his white beard, I ran to my room. I was furious. I had been lied to. The strange feeling of the insult."

It was on one of those late afternoons, on a terrace overlooking the sea in a sleepwalking snort, that you, Dana, alerted me.
"You're not here, Alan…"
And I wasn't. I was wandering far away, walking the paths of the kibbutz, then I met Professor Rosenberg, who invited me to a conversation, and asked, "Wouldn't you like to continue your studies, to do a doctorate?"
Inside, the song "I'm coming home"… Then, "My, my, my Delilah / why, why, why, Delilah…"
Again the distant voice, "We have excellent young teachers, think about it…"

You withdrew your hand, Dana. You pulled away slightly. I said that. You stared at me again, briefly asked if it was really serious that I wished to leave, as I had hinted. My silence spoke for me. You let go of me and I followed you to join your friends with whom we had gone out that night. We all continued in a simulacrum of joy.

The next morning, you called me.

You really wanted to talk, you needed to know.

"Is your mind really made up, Alan?"

I confirmed it to you. I thought I heard you breathing, Dana, until you insisted, "Do you think I have any place in your plans?"

"Archaeology, Dana, isn't that one of your big dreams? There's so much to do there! I wish we could be together all the time!"

"But the country, Alan, isn't it a little closed off? What do I know? And the religion…"

"Free, Dana, if we want to be free, accountable to no one. I love you so much. You want me to ask, to know how? For now, get your master's degree, finish your thesis as fast as you can…"

"Alan, we have so much to talk about…"

It was a holiday, and once again I went to the city, to your house. Camila received me with her affable smile; I found Lilucha in a laughing game, pretending to run away, hiding behind the furniture, then looking at me. From another room came the voice of your father, to whom I was to be introduced. He rose from his armchair in the workroom; brief words. Henrique. Untiring worker. Seminary educated, became with the years a renowned economist. Son of the regime. This is what you told me, but I'd like to know more.

The stillness, the numbness of the room.

We went down to the square. The washed and beautiful day had invited a general stampede from the city. We looked for a bench, sat there in a hug. You smiled. Between kisses, I promised you, Dana, I would know how. And it would be forever.

"And when He had gone out from there, Jesus withdrew into the region of Tyre and Sidon. And a Canaanite woman, having come out of that region, began to cry out, 'Lord, Son of David, have mercy on me. My daughter is greatly tormented by the devil.' But He answered her not a word. And His disciples, coming near, said to Him, 'Send her away, for she cries out after us.' And He answered, 'I was not sent but to the lost sheep of the house of Israel.' But she came and prostrated herself before Him, and said, 'Lord, help me.' He answered, 'It is not good to take the children's bread and cast it to the puppies.' And she said, 'Yes, Lord; but the little dogs also eat the crumbs that fall from their masters' table.' Then Jesus answered her, 'O woman, great is your faith. Be it done unto thee as thou wilt.' And from that hour her daughter was healed."

Camila had just read the text in the Gospel of St Matthew.

She looked at it once more, closed the book, placed it on a small table next to the sofa she had sat on. She faced me. Her gaze was already questioning. Then I heard it.

"Why did you ask me to read this passage?"

"This follows on from our conversation of a few days ago in which the figure of Christ was discussed, when I suggested that he was nothing more than a great reformer of Judaism."

"Because he said he had not been sent but to look after the straying sheep of his people?"

"And also because he had already stressed in another passage that he had not come to alter in any way the Law of Moses."

"Strangely enough, it is the disciples who beg him to drive away the Canaanite woman, bothering them with her lamentations."

Camila was a beautiful woman. Without difficulty, she would pass for Dana's older sister. Showing great joviality, also that afternoon when she had sat in the living room with us. Suddenly she stood up. She looked at me again. A certain restlessness in her gaze. But naturally, she said, "Next time, Alan will stay for dinner. That's settled. We'll have to go out tonight."

It was not long before Henrique entered the room. Tall, handsome, the kind of man who takes pleasure in making his shoes squeak, wrapped in an aura of sumptuousness. And with full awareness that this was so. I could perceive his falcanine gaze, hear better the austere timbre of his voice. I could detect in him a faithful and convinced defender of public order, just as it was. Then we all left. Your parents, Dana, drove on.

We stood in the square, sitting on one of those green benches, under the rumble of the sleeping city. Your eyes, your lips. The kiss.

I told you that the letter to the university had already been sent. As soon as I got an answer, you would know.

Dinner.

Everybody there. Camila, Henrique, Dana and me,

Lilucha. Grandmother Marcia retired to her room in sanctity. Your father, with a brief wave of his hand that seemed somewhat martial to me, indicated the place to his right.

The glasses, the plates, radiated a brightness that would not be everyday. Your gaze, Dana, gave off a serene contentment.

The maid, or rather the *criada*, as she was called at the time – or the "outside maid", since the other one, the "inside", was in charge of cooking – appeared, foot by foot, wearing a starched uniform, a serving dish in her hand. She approached your father – first the doctor, she had been told – immediately your mother followed her movements, controlling her, "On the left side, Laura, how many times have I told you!" Then poor Laura went round and round, looking for each one's left side.

It was your father, Dana, who imposed those first moments of studied mutism. To accentuate it, he pulled out his thick-rimmed glasses, exaggeratedly concentrated on dissecting the rock-bass, occasionally looking at us over the lenses that he had purposely let slip. With such a brief ritual had wanted to signal his austere presence and premeditated detachment. Your mother was the one who satisfied his whims, looking at him as if obeying an imperceptible baton.

Lilucha, showing signs of impatience, said, "Mama, may I speak?"

Then your father, addressing me with his voice, not his eyes, "I heard that you have just been in the Middle East."

"I went on a visit to Israel."

"And why Israel, any particular reason?"

"I wanted to meet some relatives, have a chance to get to know the country."

"You say the country, that is, the state..." – suddenly turning his aquiline gaze towards me over the hoops – "but tell me, do you find any reason why there should be a state for Jews, a state created on the basis of a religion?"

I was not surprised at the question as coming from your father, Dana; rather, I was surprised that he had considered that the proper time to formulate it.

With a certain irritation, I confess, as a boy and a young man with blood in my gills, I heard myself saying, "There was certainly no shortage of reasons for the establishment of a Jewish home, as Lord Balfour called it, and then of the State of Israel. These reasons were, moreover, added to a very large extent by the way in which other states, and I am referring to the European ones, behaved towards their citizens, for reasons, indeed, allegedly religious."

You, Dana, sitting in front of me, you would have been surprised by my throw. You touched me lightly with your foot, calming me down. But you wouldn't have been very successful.

Lilucha spoke, "Mommy, can I talk now?"

"Then I might agree with you. There have indeed been some mistakes..."

"I am sorry to contradict you, but it would be a fine euphemism to call 'errors' what have so often and repeatedly been demonstrations of genuine organised crime."

"Listen, Alan" – this was the first time that your father, Dana, had mentioned my name – "you are referring to certain states, but in a vague way, when we in Portugal, during the Second World War, behaved in, how should I say, a cooperative way?"

Laura reappeared. She began to lift plates, again under

Camila's watchful eye, but this time seeking the right side of us all.

I replied, "It is undeniable that in that period there was an important collaboration. But we must not forget the centuries of malaise, the delinquent world in which the Jewish communities lived, also in Portugal.

"What do you mean?"

"Especially the Inquisition, with all its antecedents and aftermath."

"Mama..." Lilucha tried again.

"You don't talk when adults talk," Camila told her.

"But they are always talking..."

"Elbows, miss."

Camila, turning shyly to Henrique, said, "Forgive my intrusion, but I see you are addressing a topic that deserves a long conversation. How about we leave it for another day, with more time? Alan, you have served so little!"

Then came dessert. Lilucha making faces. A strawberry slipped off her plate and fell on the white tablecloth. Henrique, rising with a certain majesty, both arms resting on the table. "I have to leave, tomorrow the board meeting; it was nice meeting you, Alan."

Then you looked at me with your sweet eyes, Dana, asking me not to be offended by your father's impetuosity. And I stared at you, wanting to apologise for my rapture too.

Then it was Camila telling me, "Alan, in your conversation with Henrique, you have touched on issues that interest me a lot. I would like to talk to you one day, you won't refuse me."

No, Dana, I will not tire you by repeating details of the

dialogue I had with your mother, because I think you will remember them. At least in part. Sitting in the living room. Grandmother Marcia, under a mantle of beatitude, nodding at her little flower *senhorinha*. You, on a low stool, roasting chestnuts in the dying fire of the fireplace. And your mother, as cheerful as she was, with her natural ease, an almost *ragazza* of our age. Inciting the conversation, we were jumping from topic to topic, with what excitement! What was not spoken of, my God! A dialogue that began on anti-Semitism, soon travelling over mountains and valleys, zigzagging at crossroads, spreading here and there, as so often happens.

The old, enthroned Christian anti-Semitism, distinct from that which sprang up in Mohammed's world, which exploded in Nazi Germany and later, that which took shape under the Communist regimes. Disorderly mention was made of the Gospels, and Luther and Wagner, and names popping up one after another. The same in literature, then appeared Shakespeare's Shylock, and Voltaire, and Céline (though there was Zola), even in Maupassant and the great Tchékhov, so I said, one finds passages in which the figure of the Jew is contemptuously addressed, and even in *The Maias* our good Eça did not shy away from repeating it, creating the figure of a servile, abject Jew, Uncle Abraão, a bric-a-brac dealer who would have nothing good but his daughter, such in the service of an impunitive rooted fashion.

"But above all, the inquisitions and mass expulsions throughout Europe, this widespread fanaticism, why?" asked Camila.

Then an essential point was referred to, the anathema of deicide cast upon the Jewish people, which gave me the opportunity to speak of the Gospels, of that one according to Matthew, of the Pauline epistles to the Romans, to the Philippians, to Titus, of the crusades, of the irresponsibility of many of the popes, of Pius XII, the one who is still to be understood, until, already almost out of time, it was the great John XIII who would have begun to recognise the nefarious crime committed by the Christian world. Above all, I pointed out, the paradox of a belief born in the name of charity and love launching itself into an ancient campaign of hatred and revenge towards a people anachronistically accused of deicide!

Until Nazism, Nazism, Nazism! When all the forces of evil were already conjured up to erupt the excrescences of a culture swollen by ancestral religious hatred, by the violence of a rude nationalism, by the motive of gluttony and rapine, easy and unpunished, by the invidiousness in the face of the success of the neighbour. And all this allied to the deep feeling of an inferior, chaotic and battered Germany, blamed for the conflict in which it had thrown Europe two decades earlier. So, once again, the awakening of the atavistically created ghost, capable of undermining a totemic world, so that its annihilation became a condition for its own survival.

"Note, Camila, anti-Semitism is a deep moral problem that the anti-Semites suffer from; it is a state of latent dementia in which they find themselves and from which they will have to free themselves. It is their problem, not ours. And believe me, I do not see any originality in this opinion on my part. Others have already said it, and I believe they are right."

The words flowed out of me with the ardour of my twenties. Your mother, Dana, didn't miss a word, she followed me eye to eye. Then it was you who came over with a plate of grey chestnuts that you had roasted by the fireplace and sat down beside us.

"So profound is the phenomenon we are talking about, Camila, that even in popular slang it manifests itself. Always and today."

"What do you mean, Alan?"

"Just take a look at one of our dictionaries and see how even these days the word Jew is still synonymous with an evil, bad-natured, materialistic, miserly individual, and that Jewry also means mistreatment, malice, mockery, derision. All this is the result of prejudices embedded in popular minds during centuries of intolerance, persecutions, malaise.

"Then there was the Dreyfus affair and the effect it had on the young Theodor Herzl, the great founder of political Zionism. I mentioned his book *The Jewish State* and, ultimately, the emergence of the State of Israel because, Camilla, contrary to what is so often said, political Zionism is not the same thing as extreme expansionism but the definitive response of a people which does not give up its right to exist in the only place to which it is atavistically attached."

"But the Arab problem, how to solve it?"

"Unfortunately, there a bubble that many have been happy to inflate. Both sides have their reasons, it is good to remember. But one thing is certain, we cannot accept an arrangement that does not imply the recognition of full and identical rights to all citizens of the country, whatever be their origins and religions. And within freely agreed borders, don't forget. Any other solution will have to arouse our repulsion. That is the only true, genuine Zionism."

Allow me, Dana, to add one more point. Surprisingly, after this conversation with your mother – has it been told? –

my relationship with your father has visibly improved. I've come to be treated with obvious familiarity. I'm sure you'll remember. Several times your parents insisted that I stay for dinner. Then we no longer went to the *boîtes* in Cascais. We stayed at home listening to records, and especially hiding cuddles. Lilucha, whenever she could, would sit on my lap and do mommies. I can't deny it, I felt good, I was already a child of the house.

We didn't have to wait long for a response from the Hebrew University. My application for a scholarship would soon be considered. As for you, Dana, they advised you to complete your master's degree first. According to the information given, there was no shortage of summer courses, also in the field of archaeology. That could be a good start for you.

A strong instinct told us we were on the right track. The kiss we didn't want to end broke up.

VI

My Home

One day you asked me, Dana, to tell you about my house. It was large and spacious, like an archipelago of secluded rooms, closed doors, isolated islets. Crossed by a long corridor lined with a red carpet that Pia walked slowly, welcoming all comers. Silence reigned.

You went there a few times, not many. It even happened that, being on my street, you didn't always want to go in.

How different our houses were from one another! In yours, we breathed an air of quietness and security, as if the whole place were in the shade of a vast and branched umbrella pine. More than once, I told you how good I felt there, though it was not always so.

I'll tell you about mine. My house. How I saw it, how I lived it. Perhaps what you will learn will help you to better judge, I'm not sure what – maybe it's just me needing to listen to myself – if what I write one day comes into your hands.

It is difficult to begin. How arbitrary it even becomes to talk about those who were close to us and bequeathed such multiple, sometimes contradictory, impressions!

Why is it that a speech, a gesture, a silence becomes more significant in our eyes than another silence, gesture or speech, when in the feeling of another they would have been understood differently, or even by us, if projected in a different light, in another context?

I'll tell you about my home from a certain family gathering. Tell you about a dinner party that was. I could do it in another way, but I believe this one will be enough. However, I do it with the certainty that the complexity of what you hear will remain sunk in me, that I still have not understood it well.

In the end will come another story that has nothing to do with said dinner, but which matters to the understanding of the house that was mine. I hope you'll stay patient, Dana.

I begin with a brief note. Although Jewish, religion had no place in our home. My mother, who had been religiously educated in a Frankfurt college in obedience to the ancestral habits and customs of the family, was not at all given to matters of ritual; my father, who often proudly evoked his origins in a rabbinical and highly regarded family of Rabat – it was even said that one of his rabbinical ancestors would have received honours of royalty on announcing his departure and entry into the city – wasted no time at all on questions of this kind. No festivals were celebrated at home – Rosh Hashanah, Hanukkah, Pesach, Sukkot or others – not even Yom Kippur*. My grandfather Richard was the only one who sporadically went to the synagogue on discreet visits.

The night we met was the first of January. Why such a date? Because of an ingrained habit, a secular ancestry. Everyone would then enjoy a natural sense of well-being; after all, the year was over and everyone was alive, hence the duty to give place to a certain joy. And the wishes and wishes that everything would be good in the coming year.

---

* On the meaning of the above-mentioned festivities, see page 123.

That's all. I'll tell you about that night, when I was a kid.

The most excited person was Pia, opening the door to everyone. From the islands she had come one day with my parents. At that hour, in a white coat freshly ironed, with her glossy hair held back with a hairpin, it was nice seeing her with her white smile shining on her Creole skin, her round and happy eyes wishing those who arrived "*âne feliz, âne feliz!*"

But there was someone who was really nervous. That was the cook, Rosa, all chubby, often in a bad mood, who by habit repelled my visits to the kitchen. The day before, I had already heard her broken record: "Hallo boy", "Go away", "Give me my place", "This is none of your business".

It was just to see the turkey.

I went in. Then I found the unlucky animal that was tumbling around in the kitchen, after Rosa had poured a few glasses of red wine down his throat; and I, who had the habit that all drunk men I met on the street always came to me, almost resented that unfortunate animal didn't pay any attention to me. Then I would see it wobbling all over while passing from one tile to the other, until it arrived at the terminal stop, its favourite one. That was the one where Rosa's round and short legs were snug, absorbed in her task of sharpening the cleaver. Until the final moment arrived, when Rosa, already saturated with my silent presence, grabbed me by the hand and pulled me away. "Get out of here, how many times do I have to say that you're only disturbing."

Here's an aside, Dana. Still about Rosa. Strange woman that one, perhaps the first person who one day came to awaken in me a curiosity for the unknowable, for the supernatural. Indeed. This was because, two or three times, I found her completely absorbed in reading and rereading some short pieces of paper that she took out of her apron pocket, her lips mulling over little secrets that only angels could hear. It was Pia who enlightened me as to the reason for that tame harangue, by saying that the other, no less, spoke to the spirits. From then on, believe me, I began to look upon her with reverential awe, for I had become aware that this bulging woman was not only an expert in fried and grilled food, but also in maintaining a speech colloquial with the otherworldly. What a great person she would have to be!

Until one day I took a chance, imagine you, and asked Rosa to tell me about the spirits, where they were and what it was like there in their world, to which she immediately threw me, "Don't bother, mind your own business."

My awe at such a portentous being lasted for some time, not long. But that's another story, for later.

Towards the end of the afternoon, a few people had already begun to arrive. Everything was ready. The big open table, white embroidered tablecloth, crockery and cutlery with the shine and elegance of a January first night. I looked at each one that came and, strangely, without finding who looked like who. This in a so-called family dinner.

An indescribable discomfort of mine. Feeling a little out of place in the middle of that adult world, then wandering around the house, aimlessly.

Also the languages. So many were spoken, sometimes it seemed that not everyone understood each other. A small babel. What was important was that when a doubt arose, someone with the key to a saving translation would jump. However, it must be said, none of that restrained anyone from drawing smiles of short duration in order to sustain the little flame of the night. Who best knew the rules of the game still must have been my father, who, perhaps by tactics, but above all by temperament, had always played at the art of contention, of saying little to say enough.

I'll tell you about my father. I have to talk about him. That night, as so often happened, he was the central figure in my eyes. Sitting at the head of the table. Spare with words, my father exuded a sober firmness that was not easy to measure.

Perhaps this came from the fact, at least as I believe, that he was a fortunate one, with something peculiar. Looking back on him today, I recall that he never experienced some of the worst griefs well known to ordinary mortals: he never suffered poverty; he never had the vexation of participating in armed conflicts (I even believe that he never entered the gates of a barracks); he never suffered the misfortune of a failed marriage or the sorrow of an ungrateful child. And if he sometimes visited hospital wards, it was because he visited indigent people who came from the islands alone to receive treatment, and my father would accompany them as if they were his family.

It is true that he had known many of life's troubles, but it is also true that they left no visible mark on him.

Continuing, my father was not a man to join groups, sects or parties, whatever their nature. He hated Salazar, nostalgically evoked some republican leaders, and never set foot in any demonstration, especially those of a pseudo-sporting or artistic nature, such as football matches and bullfights.

He did not take priests seriously, and only as a last resort would he sit before a stranger, a doctor, to litany his ailments, and even more so at his own expense.

A proud Jew – not a few times I heard him recall stories and legends of his rabbinic ancestors – far from being a synagogue man. But he acted with a religious quest for fidelity and honesty for whoever dealt with him. Pragmatically, he understood that obedience to the precepts of a faith, whatever it might be, was a matter to be decided by each one in mature age. For that reason, he imposed nothing.

My father was born on an African island bordered all around by golden sands, crowned by towering dunes where he and his little brothers would let themselves be rolled over until they plunged into the tepid green of the sea.

A little older, I imagine him tearing winds galloping on his white mare, having as a faithful friend a wolf-dog, who would throw himself into the rebellious waters when he saw him leave and who would only give up when he could no longer reach him.

He later bought a *Leica*, the first on the island, which made him an indispensable presence at weddings, christenings, birthdays and other festivities, not to mention funerals. Thus, those who wished to have a last memory of their dearly departed, arranged in a pine box and adorned with little paper flowers, he would have nothing to do but call my father.

One day, it was also his turn to buy a radio set. Still the first on the island. But no one believed that in his closed room he could listen to the conversation of someone else coming from an unknown land to pass on news to the farthest corners of the world. Moreover, in a language that nobody understood. It had to be a hoax, a mockery or, even worse, a frightening connection with beings from beyond the world.

Then my father told that for the peace of souls, one day he invited a group of the most incredulous to come to his room to witness what he was telling them. Gathered around the dubious apparatus, they sat in expectation while my father's fingers slowly turned a pulley, until, oh, God! the distant, husky voice of a BBC announcer began to sound. Then they looked at themselves with their eyes, terrified, and there were even some who started to pray to the Holy Mary, in case the speech in a strange language that came out of that macabre box was demonised.

All this my father had recalled one day, with a kind, tender smile.

I would have much to tell you of this good man, Dana, of his silent gestures of support for so many, especially when they arrived from the islands for treatment, alone and without means. Then he would seek them out, cheer them up, clothe them. And when nothing worked out, he was even the only presence at funerals. I could tell you stories. Some other time.

How different were the origins and scenarios of my mother's early childhood. With her soft blue eyes and submissive voice, my mother would take me back to her innocent days, sometimes watching her running happily through the dense forests of Schlochau and skating on the frozen lakes that surrounded the city, sometimes sliding in the snow with her parents on the sleigh ride.

She knew a lot of stories, my mother. Then, accompanying the soup that Pia always brought steaming hot, I would plunge into the fantastic, sometimes frightening world of the Brothers Grimm – *The Bremen Town Musicians*, *The Three Brothers*, the *Wolf and the Fox*, *The Fisherman and his*

Wife, The *One Who Went Looking for Fear*, *The Faithful John*. But the one I liked best and kept reminiscing about until sleep overcame me was the story of the brother and sister, Hansel and Gretel, lost in the forest, and the sorceress who wanted to devour them. Today, I believe I owe to this bizarre but beautiful tale the salutary habit of questioning a lot and, above all, of disbelieving.

Back to dinner. Everyone was already seated. It was not long before the long-awaited moment arrived when Pia came in, bringing the disgraced turkey that the day before I had met stumbling along, now naked and toasted, with legs amputated to the sides. Then he was granted a special honour, that of being deposed at the centre of a festive table. Afterwards, a new proof of appreciation was given by the way the eyes of all around were subtly focused on that outraged little body. I believe that the toasted animal may have multiplied according to the way it was seen, more greedy by some, less appetizing by others, but always looked at with curious attention.

My grandfather Richard, who only mastered the Teutonic mother tongue – and even that only when challenged, because he had long been convinced, and rightly so, that much of what is said is good for nothing – must have looked at the pussy and wondered if that was how Hedy cooked it. That's why after savouring it, slowly and meditatively, with a slight nod and brief smile, he confirmed to my mother that yes, that was how Hedy seasoned it. He would have thought of much more, certainly the family festivities, similar or otherwise, that took place at his great home, in ill-fated, shattered Germany, but that nobody could have imagined.

The one who, at least at the beginning, seemed very happy with that meeting at the first day of the year – because in these celebrations, as in others, things come in stages, the actors have their different performance times – was my Uncle Christian. Or Chris, as he preferred to be called.

I'm sorry, Dana, but I have to go a little longer on him. He deserves it, you'll see.

Danish. Protestant. He didn't speak Portuguese, as his seasons among us were usually sporadic and short-lived, but did not restrain him from distributing *obrrigadus* for the slightest gesture of courtesy that was dispensed to him, nor from weaving repeated praises to the buon vino du Porrtugal. What he couldn't stand was for even a single syllable to be uttered in the brave Germanic language. It was enough a simple *wunderbar* or *willst du?* exchanged between my mother and her sister Lotte to immediately blush. It would be his time as a resistance fighter and prisoner of war that came to his memory. You'll understand the reason for all this better in a moment, Dana.

As for his origins, I never got to know them well. I'm not sure if it was a story or just my own dream – nor does it matter, because there are so many times when the truth is more in this than in that – but the fact is that I always saw him as the son of a half-mad aristocrat living in a castle on a remote island, one of the many hundreds that make up the old kingdom of Denmark, who would one day disown him and entrust him to the care of his grandmother. She was a dry old woman of flesh and temper, who shared all her affection with a few generations of felines, all inhabitants of her noble abode. My uncle, jealous of the pussycats, would one day have kicked one of them, and the victim soon filed an appeal, and came close to his grandmother's lap. It didn't take long for the decision, which was consummated in a slap, this time on my uncle, soon put, with suitcase made, in the street. Despite the setback, Chris found shelter, got a job, sailed around the world in boats, became a brave and principled man. He saved people. He was celebrated, then forgotten. I will tell you a little more.

One day, when I was a boy of about ten, my mother took me for a tea at my uncles' house, who were in Lisbon at the time. At a certain moment, seeing me mute with boredom, it was my uncle who, with signs of a certain restlessness, turned to me and told me that today you are going to learn something. He led me to his office, with his forefinger he ordered *seat here*, leaving me there in expectation.

From a nearby drawer he took out a map, which he carefully unfolded, then he said you'll know what it was like, then we both sat side by side on a *maple*. It was about the war.

Fact is that I had heard of a war, such as the one my grandfather had been in, but when I asked him how it had been, the only answer he gave was a quick waving of his hand, tearing the air and jogging the memory, followed by a very guttural *Schrecklich!* This would be another one now, Chris's war. And I listened. He, happy at the interest with which I listened to him; I, proud of the unexpected attention accorded me.

With many erres to the mix and the necessary English canes he was telling me how the Germans leaving their house took possession of those belonging to others, destroying, pillaging, murdering. Chris was aware of a multitude of details, he knew in which month and day the Teutonic barbarians had subjugated each nation, one after another, how long it had taken the populations to capitulate and how cowardly some had come to cooperate with the invaders. And accompanying this history, there was the little map on his knees, traversed by a forefinger demarcating borders, marking intrusions. While doing so, my uncle never tired of repeating his certainty that *Germans were animals, worse than animals!*

What follows is his personal story. Enlisted among the resistance at the time of the invasion of Denmark, he blew up trains and tanks, until one day he decided to put his seafaring experience into practice. Then he devoted himself to rescue Jews, which he managed to transport to Swedish territory. He was eventually taken prisoner by the Germans, endured unspeakable violence and mistreatment, which, to his great surprise, he managed to resist.

He also showed me photos that he had taken himself at the time. To do so, he had got up and gone into a drawer to find a small red album. There you could see wrecked trains, thick smoke, a whole scene of ruin and devastation, but the most merciless were undoubtedly the living skeletons of prisoners, dressed in stripes, from which protruded a last and vain appeal in their calamitous glances. In contrast, the wolfdogs' haughty posture, at the height of their masters' polished, carded boots. As Chris passed from one photo to another, he told the story, sometimes mentioning names. Of all of them, the story that terrified me the most was that of a prisoner who, starving, had waited for the best moment to steal the bones that had remained in the guard's doghouse. But, caught in the act, amid laughter and kicks, he was grounded, chained to that miserable shelter. "*Heute habe ich ein neuer hund!*" cried the executioner, as he looked disdainfully at the prisoner turned dog.

However, as not everything in life is made up of mishaps, he recognised. I reviewed the way Chris had ended what he had just told me, drawing with his hand in the air an unexpected mini-circle of unknowable forces, to which he may have attributed the justice that one day came to be done to him. This was because in the small square where he had once gathered his Jewish refugees on their way to Sweden, a small plaque was later placed to commemorate his heroic deed.

Of all this, there remains a square named after my uncle. Those who pass by there don't even look, or if they do they soon forget. Only I remember the photos that he put in front of me, forever stuck in my memory, and that gave me an unmistakable knowledge of the stormy world that gravitated outside, beyond the walls of my house.

So, it was natural that for Chris German had become an execrable language, forbidden within a short distance from him. This is the reason why, when my mother and my aunt sometimes exchanged a word or two in what had once been their mother tongue, Chris's smiling, greedy look soon changed and flared up into a fire of anger. Aunt Lotte then turned to me, between embarrassed and laughing, with her forefinger crossing her lips to clarify softly, "*Deutsch nie und nimmer.*"

However, at dinner, Chris would have forgotten how much he had been through. With delight, he tasted the roasted turkey and gave thanks to the *buon vino rosado*. And one and one more *obrrigadu* when his glass was refilled. I looked at him from the sidelines and remembered with horror the dreadful story of the prisoner chained to the dog's hut.

Meanwhile, dinner went on with the apparent routine of these encounters of ours. Laughs, graces, sayings that not everyone understood, glasses clashing in the air in the formulation of an even vow, a laugh sounding louder. A general *adagio* with one or another note of *allegretto*.

The contrast was my father, who was particularly circumspect that night. He was a businessman, always dealing in goods that came and went from one to another country, my father lived in almost permanent anxiety. The proximate cause was some such telegrams, better said, those he waited for and sometimes didn't receive; those that came to him and he didn't always want; those that were yet to be sent. In fact, I often saw him dealing with a mini-paper that was strangely schematic in its wording, and which he once clarified to me by saying it respected negotiations, commitments to be fulfilled as rigorously and scrupulously as possible.

I confess that on that evening at the beginning of the year, my father's excessively serious air made me a little uneasy. But it all went away when at some point when my mother placed her hand on his and softly reminded him of that saying of questionable wisdom: *no news, good news*. It certainly had an effect. From then on, my father played convinced and began to intermix less silence with more smiles.

A person who was also coming was my cousin Sofia. Hostess of Sabena, she enjoyed an extraordinary charm, far more than was necessary to be accepted for the job. Straight and short hair of holly, a very clear face, splendid eyes in a strong lapis lazuli, she passed from one language to another with perfect naturalness. And as it was enough to address anyone to immediately understand the flattering thought, Sofia was prodigal in dispensing to each one a word, a brief smile. I followed her, delighted.

She was the only one that looked the turkey and its accompaniments in a more restrained manner, due to the threat that it would offer to her careful line.

It was on a flight to Rome that she met Paolo. Italian. He spoke little. If he had something to say, it was usually my cousin who did it in turn, taking his hand with a complacent smile.

But where Paolo showed himself to be opinionated was in making it clear that *si, si Napoli, Napoli,* people should not believe that it was in a small town like Verona or Siena that he was running his laundry business. *Si, si,* served by a fleet of trolleys fetching clothes and returning them duly cleaned and ironed. This was because his father, the company's founder, had made him his heir while he was still alive, in exchange for the leisure hours he spent watching *National Geographic,* stretched out in his *liegestuhl in the* shade of the weeping willow in the house's garden.

Sofia started working with Paolo, who easily infected her with the parental mania of cleaning and its benefits. Laughing to my mother, she told him that "this is our best season", and why?, "look at the red drops that you get on the towel, it's like that in every house these days". Paolo followed the conversation sphinxically until he decided to participate in the dialogue, confirming with a nod of his head that this was the case.

It remains perhaps to say that, Paolo being a Protestant by tradition, my cousin cooperated by having a prior at the wedding.

In the meantime, Pia, once everybody was served, waited on the side, her gaze saying that there was nothing left of the turkey to take to her sister Augusta, perhaps that was why her smile had waned. Unless the other, smaller one that was left in the kitchen, was roasted, she would talk to my mother about it.

Another guest was Mrs Venancia, almost a family member. Big person, with a contagious laugh, a small silver crucifix on her chest shining in her dark clothing, there was a certain nobility about her. Coming from a polished Northern family, she would never have sat on a high school bench. But this mattered little, for her studies were certainly conducted at home, of whose memory something would still remain. That is why she sometimes mentioned one or another expression in French, when by accident the term escaped her in her mother tongue, or had to display a legacy of gastronomic knowledge, if she had to invoke the esotericism of a few delicacies – some rice or tenderloin à, a partridge or a duck à, a sauce à – lest she be disgraced in the eyes of others, especially when they came from abroad. And if that was not enough to achieve her purposes, she had to resort to easy laughter, not always attentive, but which would help to cover up certain importunate gaps in time. However, in all fairness, Mrs Venancia knew the name of one or another book and its author, even if it was by the spine.

Widowed for many years by a small civil servant who was not very gifted for almost everything, she ended up as the beneficiary of a collection of creditors that only her full ears and empty purse made them give up on her. I remember that in winter we always saw her with two foxes' stoles slung over her shoulders, their flattened and pointed snouts turned backwards, and I liked to touch their little glass eyes.

As she was always happy, and that night would not be an exception, after repeatedly enjoying the meal well-watered by the assiduous and generous hand of Pia, Dona Venancia had the opportunity to recount a hilarious story that had happened to her and my mother. While she was telling it, everyone around got excited a little bit, also with the task of translating to the neighbour at the table what that good soul had to say.

If I remember correctly, it was like that. She and my mother were walking down Liberty Avenue. Suddenly, it was my mother who warned her:

"Are you noticing that there are two dogs that have been coming after us for ages?"

Moments later. "Look, now a third has joined in, and they've all started barking." Almost at once, "There's another big dog over there, it looks like it's waiting for us."

Mistress Venancia would probably be accustomed to these canine assemblies, but my mother wasn't, so, already frightened, she said, "We have to go in somewhere, I don't feel safe." And they went in the first door that was offered to them. It was in a Venice pastry shop, the one known for its *duchesses* filled with *chantilly* cream and dotted with egg threads, as Dona Venancia, with her gluttonous eyes, reminded us.

Then the waiter said, "Hey ladies, what's this all about, you barge into my house with a pack of barking dogs? I can't permit it!"

"But what do you want us to do, sir, if they come all the time after us?" argued Mistress Venancia, throbbing with tension.

Then the reply, "Well, if you come with those little foxes on your back, what can you expect? You're lucky they didn't bite them. Now turn their snouts to the front, madam. Go ahead. Out, out, out, pussy, pussy!"

"It was then that the waiter's legs and arms saved us from all that fuss, look at the mess that was there," explained Venancia, while the crucifix on her chest bounced with laughter. "There were already people getting up and dragging chairs, imagine that. Who was there, as we've seen him before, was Ferreira de Castro, yes, yes, the one from the *Round the World Tour*, with his usual melancholic look, plus a few others at the table. He stayed, he neither tugged nor mooed."

The mockery almost became generalised. Neither my father, who merely smiled, as the story was old news to him, nor my grandfather, sailing on his silent seas. Chris had taken advantage of the end of the episode and the hilarious distraction to pour himself a glass more of buon vino, and in an already known ritual did not fail to pour out a few little red drops. Pia laughed happily.

Until it was Pia's turn to start going around the table, lifting the plates. How many times my mother had told her that it was enough to look at the position of the silverware to perceive intentions, but Pia in her generosity forgot everything and asked each one "if nothing else was going". When she refused, she would smile, and after all, there was always something left to take to her sister Augusta, because Rosa hated turkey.

After toasting some sweets, everyone retired to the adjoining room. However, we had to recognise that an ineffable wave of familiarity and well-being had been generated, to which Mrs Venancia's story would certainly have contributed. It gave me the opportunity to approach my grandfather. Then it was Chris who called me to sit next to him.

Shortly after, Dana, a new act would begin. Another character would enter the scene. Someone had rung the doorbell at the entrance of the building. Pia opened it, watching who was walking up the stairs of our three floors with her regimented gait. "It's Mr David," she said, her voice already lowered with respect.

Until footsteps brought the person, and my uncle appeared. Standing up, he rested a few seconds. He entered the room, then a certain deference, although not everyone knew the reason, then kisses and hugs to the old man. On those nights, he would excuse himself from not being able to participate in the delicacies, blaming the doctors for such a sin, but he was sure to bring with him a bottle of good, genuine champagne, which he himself uncorked and distributed. After the toasts and vows were made to the tinkling of the glasses, my father and uncle retired to a corner of the room, where David's cigar was perfuming the room.

All the others continued in their entertaining chatter, in a multilingual and giggling chat.

My grandfather had taken advantage of a moment of general distraction to silently return to his room. No one had noticed anything but my mother, who followed him later, confirming that everything was fine.

It didn't last until everyone was gone.

Allow me, Dana, to spread myself a little, by telling of this uncle of mine, who was already my father's, made among us, and not only, a bit of a legend.

He was in his seventies, but still well built. Tall, corpulent, a slight curve assured him of a measured physical superiority over the others. He exuded an ineffable aura of energy; without presumption, he knew how to command.

I remember in him some traits that always attracted and intrigued me. First of all, the searching gaze of someone who had lived a long life and did not shy away from anything. Then, his sonorous voice, his typical Sephardic *facies*. And the gold chain in a bow on the vest of the grey suit. The truth is that I had never seen him wearing anything other than that colour suit. He was a figure that denoted firmness, a natural dignity.

I, a child, looked at my uncle with admiration – because there were many stories that were already told in his time – although it seemed to me that he did not want me near him. I think he disliked me. Nevertheless, when he returned from the islands and appeared at our house, it was known and certain that at some point, already well installed on the sofa in the living room, he would call me with his forefinger, "Come here, boy!" I was already waiting for the moment to come. He would soon take a coin from his vest with a dry and resounding "Take it!" That's how I got in my hands, on a few occasions, the silver effigies of Charles I, King, and Amelia, Queen of Portugal. As I already knew the royal features, without wasting time I would run with the coins to my room and let their majesties slip through the slot of my small savings box.

Other times, I received little gold coins with profiles of different royalties, and not only, but without making distinctions, to all I gave the same luck, letting them fall through the narrow opening of my savings prison. Afterwards, I entertained myself rattling the box with that cash; it was fun to hear the noble laughter, or perhaps the protests that went on inside. Until the day came when I began to think about what I was going to do with my captives. So, I asked my father if there was a way I could exchange that court of monarchs and dignitaries for real money, that what I wanted was to buy a bicycle. My father nodded yes. Said and done. I put my little piggy bank spewing out the beautiful aristocracy that had been imprisoned, and once freed I put it in order according to the diameter of the coins, without looking any further. I immediately called my father, who took them away. Thus, a couple of days later, I received in exchange a considerable wad of notes, already plebeian money, the kind my mother used to go shopping with. With it, I made my first investment and one of my life's dreams. I went to a shop in the Rato area, handed over some paper and got a bicycle.

Still about my uncle. Stories and legends were told about him. A great and domineering figure, he came to fulfil the functions of a real sheriff on the island. He was the authority.

They say he started out as a boat captain. True or a lie? I don't know. I was also told – I am not sure whether I heard or dreamed, which is not important in this case because I am used to accepting daydreams without questioning them in vain – that one day his sailboat was attacked by a band of pirates in the middle of the sea and they took him prisoner and even condemned him to death. But my uncle, with his innate sharpness, found a way around it – how, I can't tell – until they let him go free on a barge. As a present they gave him a compass.

Let it dawn and hit land.

After such an adventure, David decided to leave the seas, opened a business, managed his warehouse. If there was no teacher at school, it was he who taught the first letters; he became an expert in resolving disputes. Was there a fight between two people? Then the best thing to do would be to look for "Nhô" David, who would play the judge, he would decide who had the right.

He came to have many barges with which he carried salt from the island, which became a fruitful business, and two-masted schooners running around the archipelago. There must have been more than twenty of them. To make fun of himself and others, he gave them stupid names – *I don't know*, *Which*, *Maybe*, *Like this* – so that someone who sent a letter informing a relative that he would arrive on such and such a day on the *I don't know* or the *Maybe,* or any other ship with a similar name, would soon make those who received the letter suspect that it was written after having drunk so many grog. But there was also the *Sal-Rei*, a pretty little sailboat with only one mast, which my uncle had ordered from abroad and which he kept for himself on his rounds of the islands. When he went in it, he went alone, with the crew.

It is also said of the peculiar way "nhô" David ran his business. He bought whatever they came to sell him, and sold whatever they wanted to buy. His warehouse was full of the most varied merchandise, as if he predicted that the years of penury would come knocking at the door. Who knows if he acted thus, fruit of atavistic, biblical reminiscence of the dream of the Pharaoh and what Joseph said, warning him to take heed, for the seven years of plenty would be followed by seven years of famine?

David was not wrong. So when drought struck the islands, bringing death to tens of thousands of inhabitants, David did not rest. All his efforts were so that not one of the islanders died of starvation. He made sacks and sacks of corn, flour, beans and who knows what else reach remote villages. Had it not been for his care, the luck would have been quite different, because there was no one else who could provide assistance to the population. Not only that. Since my uncles, David and his wife Gigi, lived in a big house in the centre of the village, it was certain that anyone who came from a distant village and needed an inn would have to knock on the door. There was no lack of mattresses in the vast two-storey house.

With Aunt Gigi, the fact is that things didn't always seem to go well. From time to time, there was a quarrel. It is said that at meal times they sat at the table far apart, annoyed with each other, without exchanging a word. They communicated by means of little notes, sending them by the hand of the maid who served them, with a warning: "Take them to Mrs Isabel", "Give them to Mr David". To ensure such a lively dialogue, I would like to believe that each of them would have a notepad and a sharp pencil next to the spoon.

What would those two say through the little papers scribbled there? Since in truth they always had been friends, maybe it was just the question, "David, are you enjoying the cachupa?" And the answer, "Gigi, if you added a pinch of paprika, sweet chili and cassava, it wouldn't be bad at all."

I could tell you so much more about my uncle, Dana! If I had the skill to do it, I would dedicate a whole book to him, because he deserves it. Especially since he's been a great benefactor. But one more still follows.

Although a vernacular Jew in character and features, one day he decided to build a beautiful chapel on top of a hill, an offering to Gigi, a believing Catholic, who used to pray there. Inside, he had it decorated with beautiful frescoes, and from the mainland he ordered an image of Our Lady of Fatima. It was not long before the chapel of Fatima became a place of worship for anyone from the island, a meeting place, a place for festivities and processions.

But with his ancestral practical sense, as he understood the shortness of the days, David came to make use of a small plot of land a little far from the village, which belonged to the family. In it, he buried his father and mother, under tombstones ordered from outside, with their sayings in holy language. Other relatives and himself were also buried there, all on similar stelae, whose sacred writings none of them could decipher.

Today, there it is, the Jewish cemetery of the island, a small and modest place, walled and with a closed door, attesting in its secular mutism, traditions and cultures of people who came from abroad to stay, live, serve.

I had told you at the beginning, Dana, that some other things would follow which have nothing to do with the January first dinner, but which matter so much to my household.

It's my turn to tell you. It's about Pia.

One day, see what I decided to do. To talk about religion, a subject that was not a topic of conversation at home. We practised a morality of good behaviour, that was unbreakable, objective, without beating about the bush. Cults? None. Then I decided to ask Pia, me a little boy around the size of the waist of a man.

"Pia, what's your religion?"

"What do you mean?" she asked.

"Look, we're Jewish. Chris says he's Protestant, but I don't know what that is, Aunt Gigi even has a chapel, Rosa only believes in spirits. And what are you?"

"Me? Nothing."

"What do you mean, nothing? What do you believe?"

"I believe in all the saints, amen, but more in Santa Barbara. They say she is stronger, the one who helps the most."

"Then why do you say you're nothing?"

"I wasn't at church, so there's no baptism."

This conversation left me confused. Pia had no baptism, so she was nothing. Well, neither had I been baptised, but I had never been told I was nothing. I had always heard that we were Jewish.

My father gave me a very short, but quite eloquent answer, when one day he took me to his office, in Rua do Alecrim, the very steep one that goes from Camões to almost the river, and in a pause in which he stopped typing the old *Royal*, glasses on his forehead, after he gave me time to ask.

"Dad, what's all this about religions, about some being baptised and others not, Chris is Protestant, we Jews?"

"Hey, son, cut the crap. Be good, do your best, help others. And above all, don't lie or steal. The rest is bullshit."

"Is that why we are Jews and the others are not?"

"Our families already were. One day, all that will be clear to you."

This was the very short dissertation I received from my father, as was his wont. Immediately, his spectacles fell from his forehead and *Royal* returned to its rhythmic talk. My father's tranquillity had really calmed me down. So because he had just said that lying was forbidden.

One summer we happened to spend a few days at Bom Jesus do Monte. We had been there before, and I remembered with tension those many little chapels all along the staircase.

What I could never forget was the image of that huge and bloody Christ crucified at the entrance of the sanctuary, and inside the bones of a Saint Clement, protector of hernias, gathered under an old lace, in a glazed tomb. And the green lake surrounded by an extensive, dense park.

Sometimes, at night, I would dream about all this. Until the day came. We went on, in our Black *Hudson*, the GH-14-11. I was sitting with Pia in the back seat. Closed to herself, she was smiling. She seemed far away, absent, but happy. There was something different about her that I hadn't known before. Later, I realised she was already coming up with a secret idea.

Until we arrived. The Hotel do Elevador. Along the façade a ream of wicker chairs, a few guests sitting there, mumbling. Among them were two old ladies. One more than the other, the older one with a rosary twirling between her fingers.

Two or three days later, I was leaving the hotel with Pia to go to the park when she said to me, "Wait a little." Then she approached the two ladies and I heard their conversation.

Like this:

— "Good morning, ma'am. You'll excuse me, but I have a question."

This with the less elderly one. The other had not noticed anything.

"Say it, dear."

"I don't know, but there must be a priest here at the convent."

"Of course, there is always a priest in the shrine, it's Father Hilario. And why do you ask that?"

"If possible, I need to talk."

"Who do you need to talk to? If it's the priest, you can go to the shrine and look for him. But let me ask you now, what do you want from the priest?"

"It's that I have no baptism. They didn't give baptism. If possible, I can take it now."

"Oh dear, so you're not baptised? Jesus Christ! Holy Mother of God! That's a sin! Listen, do you want me to tell the priest about you?"

"If you please."

"Dear daughter, I'm very happy to do this for you. Look, my name is Eugenia, and this lady is my mother. I'm still going to speak to Father Hilario today."

Next, we went to the lake in the park to paddle. I had never seen Pia so happy. A serene and deep smile was stamped on her face, then we started paddling each on our own side, but we did it haphazardly, splashing each other on purpose, laughing like children of the same age. In the following afternoons, Pia disappeared somewhat mysteriously. I wanted to know where she was going, but Pia answered me silently. It was my mother who warned me, "Let her go, she's going to the church to meet the priest to learn how to pray, don't keep asking questions." And I didn't ask any more questions.

One day, Pia informed me that *"sinhô padre"* wanted to talk with me, then she asked me to come to the temple.

I went. Father Hilario told me that Pia was going to be baptised in the next few days, he wanted to know if at the baptism ceremony I would be ready to carry a silver cross with the crucified Christ. I asked him if it was OK, because I was not baptised. The priest told me that it was Pia's wish, he also reassured me by telling me that one day the Lord would also call me, and with so many certainties I could only say yes.

Until the moment came. Mrs Eugenia, with a dark veil on her head, played the godmother. Pia, covered with another veil, but white, looked beautiful. My mother was the one who was anxious, she had to go at Pia's insistence, but without experience of those events, she was afraid that people would have to kneel down, then she would not know where to stand. I was put in front of everyone holding aloft a silver Christ about my height, behind came Father Hilario trilling a weeping chant in a strange language that was none of my home. Suddenly, I turned and saw the Creole face of Pia shining wet, Father Hilário always insisting on a sad speech of another world, all that in a sluggish pace under the flickering light of the temple. Christ began to weigh me down, until we reached the baptismal font. Finally, I was able to set him down on the ground, so He and I both stood waiting side by side, me taking a deep breath.

Standing there with my alert ear, even though I did not understand a word of what Father Hilario's loud voice announced while he was sprinkling Pia's head. I saw them all crossing themselves. Mrs Eugenia smiled piously; my mother, static, gave signs of commotion; I just wanted it to end and for us to return to normality.

When the time came, everything was over, but normality had changed, because Dona Eugenia, who had always treated

Pia as her daughter, had kissed her and started calling her her sister.

A few days later, the holiday was over, but don't think, Dana, that it all ended in sanctity.

We had arrived home – at the time we lived near the penitentiary – when the very next day Mrs Maria, the doorkeeper, came to my mother.

"I have to talk to you, ma'am."

"What's the matter, something wrong?" my mother asked.

"It's such a subject, I don't really know how to begin."

"Go ahead, Mrs Maria, be my guest."

"Oh, ma'am, it's Rosa."

"What's with Rosa?"

"It was my António who saw him come in, he knows him well, he was the jailer there, Constâncio. My António goes and asks him, 'So, you're here?' and he says he's visiting his cousin, Rosa, who he hasn't seen for a long time. But the scene was repeated more times, then I found him leaving in the morning, so I thought I should warn you."

When Pia knew what happened, and even that Rosa had not denied it, she loudly declared that what Rosa had done must have been almost a mortal sin. It is certain that, whether Pia was right or not, Rosa finally returned to her village, and the spirits with which she entertained herself chatting were of no use to her.

Conclusion, after coming from Bom Jesus do Monte, Pia returned somewhat sanctified, the other left sacrilegious.

There were times, Dana, when we talked about our families, our homes. How different they were! In yours, it is well known, a profound calm reigned, an ineffable serenity coming from the earth as from heaven. Your old grandmother, with her rosaries and endless prayers carried and brought messages from the divine. Your father was the one who assured the earthly well-being, that of the present and of the possible tomorrow. Your mother, affable, cautious, always a master in reconciling the commands of heaven with the minutiae of earth.

My home was another one. I would say, a collage of very diverse portraits, in a setting made fragile by the variety of traditions, and past, languages and faith. Remnants of Babel? In it blew fires of life, fumes of death, silent explosions of laughter and pain, it was the fantastic house that made me and from where one day I left taking with me the ghost that is of me.

My home always seemed to me like a boat coming from afar that some had brought, castaways who had learned to turn sails and had become captains of the high seas.

VII

Judaism – A Brief Note

One day, Dana, you asked me to talk to you about Judaism. It was a subject which occasionally came up in conversation, even in your house, and of which little was known. I would like to be able to do it. But lest you say I didn't try, here follows a brief passage, following a course that was mine.

I was in the first year of high school. Among the subjects I was especially curious about was the one called moral and religion, or vice versa, I don't remember well.

Once a week, the bulging figure of Father Guilhermino appeared there, wearing a black cassock and white collar, who immediately impressed me by uttering one of the most intriguing sayings I had ever heard: in his classes we would listen to the word of God. In order to do so, he ordered us to come with a *Bible*, the *New Testament*.

I said it at home, and it was with a certain diffidence that my mother and I went into a downtown bookshop to buy the book. To our surprise, they didn't have it at the moment, but they could order it. We went to another specialised bookshop and then I bought it.

It was a beautiful little book, with a red cover, it looked like it was made of cloth, and I was dying to get home, eager to start leafing through it. Being a book of divine inspiration, according to the wise warning of Father Guilhermino, was there anything that could compare to it? That is why I began to hold my *Holy Bible* with much greater veneration.

At home, in the room alone, it didn't take long for the dazzle to set in. What enthusiasm I had. First the apostille of a canon with a strange saying, *nihil obstat*, and another from a bishop mentioning an *imprimatur*, things that immediately demanded respect; then a letter from the Vatican, signed by a cardinal, sent in the name of the Holy Father congratulating the publication of that little-great work I was holding in my hands; inside, multiple and sombre drawings in black ink, some of men looking holy, others in a pose of adoration; at the end, an index of everything that was there, the *Gospels*, there were several of them, the Acts of the Apostles, the Epistles, so many, to the Romans, to the Corinthians, to the Galatians, Ephesians, Philippians, Colossians, Thessalonians, and more, and more, my God, so many things I had never heard of! Finally, the Apocalypse of St John.

Half hidden, almost unnoticed, were the folded pages of a small map, under the title "Palestine at the time of Jesus Christ", so that it would be impossible to raise doubts about the sanctity of that little book that was now mine.

Then began the lessons of Father Guilhermino. Gradually, he read to us in a dramatically attuned voice the first *New Testament* passages, they were from the *Gospel* according to St Matthew.

I was immediately amazed by the historical knowledge with which the genealogy of Jesus was fixed, generation after generation, going through King David until arriving to Abraham; I found the story of the conception and birth of Christ touching, as well as the adoration of the Magi, but, I confess, then came the disturbing flight to Egypt. Why the flight? It was Herod who, fearing the birth of the King of the Jews, had ordered the killing of all the children from two years old and under in Bethlehem and its surroundings, thus giving rise to the sadly proclaimed death of the innocents.

I remember that this incident after the birth of Jesus caused me an unexpected apprehension, which I could perhaps express thus: the coming of the Saviour would immediately become the cause of the death of many other children – how many? – without any harm coming from them. What is the reason for this apparent injustice? Because I did not inquire, I was left without knowing why.

Then comes the preaching of John the Baptist in the desert of Judea, clothed in camel skins, feeding on locusts and wild honey, to whom many from Jerusalem and all Judea flocked to be baptised by him in the Jordan River. It was at this passage that things began to change for me from doubt to amazement. This because the angry voice of the preacher, who, seeing many Pharisees and Sadducees coming to his baptism, said to them:

"Brood of vipers, who taught you to flee from the wrath that threatens you? (...) Every tree therefore that does not bear good fruit will be cut down and thrown into the fire."

At that time, I asked the good priest Guilhermino what was that about Pharisees and Sadducees. He explained to me that those were the Jews, and that, as the holy book said, like the trees that do not bear good fruit, they would have the destiny of the eternal fire. I heard him with stuporous fright, astonishment that left me numb, then, already at home in my closed room, I started to leaf through the little red book with even more eagerness, a very rare anxiety, it was a silent meeting between my book and me. Once again, I stopped before the *nihil obstat* and the *imprimatur*, sayings that would certainly attest to the fact that it was a work of transcendent scope and truth; to confirm it, there followed the letter sent in the name of the Holy Father, but holy why? I asked myself, it was not that saints are only after death – the bones of St Clement, protector against hernias or breaks, whom I had once known in the monastery of Bom Jesus, jumped out at my eyes – but the one in the book was still alive and sending missives, but I did not dare ask Father Guilhermino for clarification, because in class no one asked anything.

Closed to myself, I would read passages and more passages from the *Gospel*, some of them non-stop readings, others in a skipped way, and, from time to time, in a repeated confirmation, I would come across serious accusations addressed to those Sadducees and Pharisees, in a word, to the Jews. They were thus, "Brood of vipers how can ye say good things, ye who are evil?" "Woe unto you, scribes and Pharisees, hypocrites!" "Give no heed to Jewish fables, nor to the commandments of men who are departed from the truth... They confess that they know God, but they deny him with their works, being abominable, and rebellious, and incapable of every good work." "Serpents, brood of vipers! How shall ye escape the damnation of hell?" And that was not all.

The more I read, the more disorientated I became. At a certain moment, it was panic that took hold of me, such was the case when, one day, Father Guilhermino, with a smile on his face, went from one desk to the other handing out a prayer booklet to each of the children, where, oh, my God! clearly illustrated the destiny of all souls in the next world. Soon, my eyes were fixed on four illustrations in coloured squares, they were drawings of Heaven, Purgatory, Limbo and Hell. Among the four, of course I jumped to the last one. There I saw myself, licked the whole body by eternal flames. What's more, now it all seemed to make sense. Thus, you see, when the wise Priest Guilhermino came to know that I had not been baptised, he immediately alerted me to the risk in which I lived, nothing less than that of finding myself in mortal sin, which was in accordance with what came in the little red booklet, repeating insistent curses against those who were not, and informing what it would be afterwards. Until that brief primer came to my hands proving by a+b that the destiny of whoever had led such a highly sinful existence as mine would be to serve as pasture to the infernal flames. I was lost, Father Guilhermino had reminded me that the simplest burn already hurts so much, imagine what the whole body will be forever made pasture for the fire.

It was worth the Christmas holidays. I stayed home with nothing to do, bothering my mother, who then asked my father to take care of me. He agreed, my thanks to him! So, he took me to his office in Rua do Alecrim – I think, Dana, that more than once I have mentioned this episode to you that I never tire of evoking – there I entertained myself in the mornings opening drawers and cupboards, hitting keys on a typewriter, in a word, pestering those who worked there, but it was on one of those days that I decided to stand up to him, because, truth be told, I tended to blame my father for the unmeasured and perpetual punishment that was already destined for me.

I firmly entered his office, sat down on a sofa in front of his desk, but my father didn't even notice me, absorbed in drumming his fingers on his old Royal. The skill and concentration with which he did it gave me an unforgettable astonishment, he emanated unusual competence and security in the way he worked without needing anyone, while I stood there, crumpled, frightened by things I had heard. But I didn't give up.

I waited for the pause that was sure to come, it was the moment *Royal* was silent, my father raised his glasses, held them on his head, looked at me, then I attacked him. I poured out everything I had heard from Father Guilhermino and what I had read in the little red booklet. Finally, I told of the terrible images of the primer I had been offered, everything in conformity, I had to vent my panic. I waited for the answer, what would my father have to say? Then it came short, sharp, blunt, as it had already happened on other occasions. "Bullshit, my son, don't pay any attention. Behave, do your best, help the others whenever you can, the rest is just a song."

Almost at once, his spectacles fell from his head, my father gave a little touch to the faithful Royal, which soon resumed its metallic singsong.

Faced with this, I had no choice but to choose between two truths, that of the priest Guilhermino and the *Gospel*, which even included a letter from the Holy Father, and that of my father, announced one morning in his office at Alecrim Street. The choice was not difficult for me, I definitely voted for the second one.

From then on, everything changed. After the holidays, and back to religion classes, I was already a different boy. While Father Guilhermino preached his litanies and judged the future in the other world, I, without paying attention, opened the small map of Palestine attached to the red booklet, staring at it. Then I would let my finger guide me down it, from Sidon to Tyro, to Mount Carmel, Nazareth, Caesarea,

Jaffa, Gaza. Once there, I would go up by Hebron, I strolled along the Dead Sea, I continued through Bethlehem and Jerusalem, I came close to the Jordan River, I continued northwards, Mount Tabor, Tiberias, Capernaum, so that, I confess, as often as I made these pilgrimages, all those places that had been strange became familiar to me.

Sometime later, not long, something happened, Dana, that is important for me to tell you. Given my habit of snooping in drawers, bookshelves, closed cupboards – which came to an end when I found myself alone at home – one day, amidst a lot of books, I came across a blue-covered, hard-bound volume, a little thicker than the little red book. I open it. This was a strange book, on each page two columns of text, one in Portuguese, the other in unknown characters, which I came to know were Hebrew. What could it be about? Nothing less than the Law of Moses! The *Torah*! The *Pentateuch*! That's what the cover said. To confirm, the index indicated its five books, *Genesis*, *Exodus*, *Leviticus*, *Numbers*, *Deuteronomy*, of which, in truth, I had heard little or nothing about. But for my peace of mind, at the bottom of each page, a commentary on what was there. As I was later told, this was the main book of the Jews, those Pharisees and Sadducees who were reviled to death in that little red book. I was very interested to know what my blue book had to teach. But that was not the only reason for my curiosity, another was because I had heard one day that Jesus had not come to the world to abolish the old law, but rather to fulfil it. That is why I definitely had to know the old law, which was already in my hands at that time. I kept it with the utmost piety.

In the evening, already in bed, I began to read *Genesis*. The first verses told stories that were not unknown to me, such as the creation of the heavens and the world, of light and darkness, of man made of the dust of the earth, whom God had placed in the garden of Eden, then the disobedience in eating from the tree of the garden, until the great punishment when the waters of the flood rained down. The story of Noah, a just man, and his family, charged to preserve any creature in which there was the spirit of life, this one I read and reread ecstatic, such was the enchantment. In it, I found a strange beauty that deeply resonated in me, and encouraged me to continue. Then, for my peace, I read something else, that the Eternal had intended a covenant, not only with good Noah, but with all that came from him, even with all the animals that came out of the ark.

He said, *"And I, behold, I establish my covenant with you, and with your seed after you. And with every living soul that is with you (...) every one that came out of the ark, every beast of the earth (...). I have put my rainbow on cloud, and it shall be for a sign of a covenant between me and the earth."*

It did not take long before I reached the Lech Lechah verses, which tell of Abraham and his descendants; in this *Parasha* I paused without being able to move forward, because I had already related what I had learned in the little red book with what the *Torah* now told me. The first one taught me the genealogy of Jesus, son of David, son of Abraham, the same one with whom, the *Torah* clarified, the Eternal signed a special and eternal alliance.

"And Abraham was ninety-nine years old, and the Eternal appeared to him and said to him: I am God Almighty; walk before me and be perfect. And I will make my covenant between me and you, and I will multiply you exceedingly. (...)

And I will make my covenant between me and thee, and between thy seed after thee, throughout their generations, in an everlasting covenant, to be thy God, and thy seed after thee."

This being so, it left me in no doubt that I had come across two sacred texts propagating truths that appeared to me to be incompatible. While the oldest, *Genesis*, insistently evoked the covenant not only between God and man and every living soul, but also another to be added between the Almighty and Abraham and those who came from him, a covenant to be in force forever and ever, the *Gospel* that Father Guilhermino was keen to read to us considered those born of Abraham's seed as hypocrites, wicked, serpents. Then I wondered if that was so. Would the Eternal have wanted to enter into an alliance with people who were nothing more than a race of vipers, incapable of good work, whose fate would be, after all, damnation to the flames?

Here, Dana, is the outline of one of the greatest doubts I have ever had. No, I will not tire you with the after. I will tell you, in simplicity, that a new window was being drawn for me, and that, with cost and time, I opened it. I have succeeded only a little. And from what I have been able to infer, what follows are some unpretentious and disorderly lines.

Sigmund Freud, whom I take for an unsuspected observer, once wrote words that touched me deeply, they met what in a vague way I felt and held.

He confessed that he was as far removed from the Jewish religion as from all the others, considering them as mere objects of scientific study. Freud recognised that, in spite of his poor knowledge of Hebrew language and literature, he had a very strong feeling of community with the Jewish people.

It is clear that Sigmund Freud not only did not practice, but was also unaware of the intricacies of religion, which did not prevent him from feeling a close bond with a people with whom he identified. A similar statement may be attributed to many, many other Jews. Hence, we may state that it is not necessarily in the observance of the Jewish religion, nor even in its knowledge, that the essence of feeling resides.

Next, after relegating the religious element as defining Judaism (although he lamented its unpreparedness and religious unculture) Freud points out, as we have seen, the importance of a feeling of community with a people he considers his own. In other words, for Freud the concepts under analysis – Jew, Judaism – are not necessarily centred on a sacred reality, but are susceptible of coming from another one, of a profoundly secular nature, which is the idea of identity with a people.

In taking that attitude, Sigmund Freud has not simplified the issue. He has complicated it, but in doing that, Dana, I think he has come close to the truth. At least what I think is the truth.

Then it will be asked: what people, what community is this, so widespread throughout the world, and how can we find and define it if we dissociate that people from the religion which for millennia it has professed? What will remain if such a disconnection is made? And where to seek the unifying, defining element of that same people? Because it will certainly exist, and only by detecting it will we understand the reason for its permanence in the course of a history so full of misfortunes. Freud has touched on a rather nebulous question, but I believe that in doing so, he supported something very significant.

In order to explain the enigmatic character of the Jewish people and its subsistence to the present day, Freud believes that it was the man Moses that moulded such character by giving to his people a religion which exalted a high degree of self-esteem, causing enormous progress in spirituality and opening the way to the valuation of intellectual work.

What a great distance there is between Freud, who tried to understand the idiosyncrasies of the people to whom he felt attached, going back to events of millennia ago, and Sartre, for example, who with unusual levity maintained something quite different, that it was the others who had given rise to the character that the Jewish people assumed throughout history.

According to Sartre, Christians are responsible for Jewish subsistence by preventing assimilation of the Jewish people. In the final analysis, in his opinion, a Jew is a man considered as such by another man. Nothing more than that.

Only an abyssal ignorance of Jewish essentiality can lead to such statements. It is forgotten that the foundations of Judaism are in the *Torah*, the Law of Moses, dictated and fulfilled millennia before the emergence of Christianity and before anti-Semitism was unleashed in the world.

Christianity and anti-Semitism, Dana, were undoubtedly exogenous factors determining the crystallisation of a certain type of Jewish behaviour, and above all the way in which the Jew came to be regarded by others, but this has nothing to do with the inner truth, the depth of the spirituality of this people which enabled it to go forward and overcome the unspeakable obstacles it had to face.

Strange as it may seem, I think Freud touched on the heart

of the matter by pointing to the teaching of Moses as the foundation on which the essential pillars of Judaism have rested over millennia, and which has led, as Freud indicated, to enormous progress in the realm of spirituality and the great appetite for the work of the mind.

Once I have reached this point, Dana, and trusting your patience, I proceed in seeking to understand how much can be drawn from the aforementioned assertions of Sigmund Freud.

The God who will appear on Mount Sinai is a God who does not make his face known, for He said, *"You shall not be able to see my face, for man cannot see me and live... And I will remove my glory afterwards, and you shall see my back, and my face shall not be seen"* (*Exodus* – 33: 20, 23).

Not only a God who is unseen, but also difficult to name. Hence the various ways in which he is invoked – Adonai, Ashem, Elohim, Iié Asher Iié, and above all by the unreadable tetragram YHWH.

Here, it seems to me, is, in brief reference, the starting point of the profound revolution brought about in the world by the message of Moses: the belief in the oneness of a God who is totally abstract, and who contacts a single people in order to enter into a covenant with them. Then Moses said to the Eternal, *"And thus shall we be distinguished, I and thy people, from all the peoples that are upon the face of the earth"* (*Exodus* – 33:16), to which he was answered, *"This also that thou hast spoken, I will do; for thou hast found favour in mine eyes, and I have known thee by thy name"* (*Exodus* – 33: 17).

It is in this singular pact, which will come to question the polytheistic beliefs of that time, that most probably underlies the ancestral animosity towards the Hebrew people, elected to awaken such a revolutionary understanding of the divine. This animosity, Dana, will increase when this same people reject the idea propagated by the man Yeshua (Jesus) that He would be the Son of God. Accepting Him would mean breaking the divine covenant with YHWH, the one God who does not want to be seen and represented. The man Yeshua, despite having stated that he would not alter Moses' words in any way, would not have taken into account the fact that the high spirituality with which the Mosaic God was conceived was not compatible with the vulgarly human concept of paternity. The cut between Judaism and Christianity became irreducible when, later on, to this fundamental deviation, the belief in the Holy Trinity was added, as it results from the Scriptures (Matthew 28:19). Reconciliation between Mosaic Unitarianism and Christian trinitarianism will become impractical; both will pursue their paths throughout history, each on its own.

Allow me, Dana, to go on a little further.

Jewish Unitarianism will have profound repercussions in the field of ethics. The alliance celebrated on Mount Sinai obliged the Hebrew people to fulfil commandments, *mitzvot*, of two fundamental kinds: commandments concerning the relationship between God and man and those reflecting the relationship between man and his fellow man.

The main source is the Decalogue received on Mount Sinai; there it explicitly enumerates the man's principal duties towards God, and those which are imposed on man's living together with his neighbour. It is interesting to note that the latter group includes six out of the ten. However, those duties do not lose their religious character, but rather take on a fundamental importance. That is why, when a pagan who wanted to become a Jew asked the elder Hillel what was the essential of the doctrine, he would have answered him: Do not do to others what is hateful to you, everything else is commentary.

Such in accordance with Leviticus (19: 18) which commands, "You shall love your neighbour as yourself."

The centrality of the human person in Judaism can be seen in a different light, when duties towards another are breached. In such a situation, notwithstanding the divine character of the duty, forgiveness is not conferred by God unless it has also been given by the offended party, who is the one who has the last word. Here, Dana, is a striking note of distinction between the Jewish absolution and the same according to the Christian confession.

Even on the day of Yom Kippur, the Day of Atonement, on which the Jews ask for remission for their offenses against the divine law, offenses committed towards another will not be excused if he himself has not granted their forgiveness.

But forgiveness must be given by the victim if the offender sincerely asks for it.

Lévinas recognised it when he expressly maintained that even God may not forgive an offense committed by a man towards his fellow. The contrary would be inhuman.

In this way, I believe, Dana, we see a singular manifestation of human dignity, even in the face of divine omnipotence. This is a particular space in which man is the sole master of his person, judge of a wounded dignity, holder of the indelible and unrestrained power to forgive.

No, Dana, still on the subject of *mitzot*, it should be clarified that these are not merely meditations, thoughts and other reveries, notwithstanding the relevance of the intentional element, the *kavanah*. *Mitzvah* that does not manifest itself in terms of action is *mitzvah* that did not come into the world, because it was not fulfilled. The duties of solidarity and social justice, so well emphasised in literature and well known in the Jewish world, find their source here.

Moreover, Dana, knowledge of the *mitzvot* – which not only concern man's duties to God and his neighbour, but also his obligations to himself, to the land he toils on, to the animals that do it with him – is attainable only through the study of the *Torah* (a word meaning teaching), which is itself already a *mitzvah*.

Because education through research constitutes a cornerstone of Judaism, Freud's statement that the Mosaic religion was the door that opened the way to the valorisation of intellectual work is understandable.

One further point to note, Dana: knowledge will not be based on what is literally said in the *Torah*, because it requires techniques of rabbinic interpretation that lead to adding to the biblical text rules of oral tradition contained in the monumental work that is the Talmud. To the point that, Rav Kook recalls that the *Talmud* goes so far as to declare that *Chacham adif mi'navi*, meaning that the rabbi is preferable to the prophet. Why is this so?

Who could imagine that thousands of years later rabbis are those who dedicate their lives to the study of the *Torah* and education of the Jewish people, thus removing idolatry and the various sources of oppression.

So much, so much more there would be to say, Dana, and the thought alone almost paralyzes me, for all that I would add would mean little or nothing.

As a religion, but a philosophy of life as well, Judaism does not stop, but rather encourages free discussion. If this is so in the *Torah* itself, where man freely dialogues and questions with the divine, how could it not be so in the inter-human relationship? Perhaps in this remote source, we can find the ancestral curiosity, the propensity for study and research, with its marked mark of boldness, sometimes even irreverence, constituting inalienable ingredients of the Jewish attitude. From here to the well-known *chutzpah of* the man of today and of always, the distance will not be long.

It is not difficult to believe, therefore, that there are many opinions about divinity. If for some He is the great creative force to whom man addresses his prayers, as Maimonides considered it, for others He is the One who vibrates in each molecule of the universe, according to a Spinozian conception, or even the One who erases Himself from human eyes, in order to overvalue the inter-subjectivity of *Ich und Du*, in the existentialist vision of Martin Buber. But whatever conception one has, what does not change are the unbreakable rigours of ethics, which make Judaism a living humanism.

As a people, the Jews have an all afflicted history of events from which they almost miraculously escaped, and which came to be celebrated and remembered as lessons in life. Celebrating memory has always been a duty. To this end, let us point to Pesach, remembering the liberation from slavery in Pharaoh's time; Shavuot, commemorating the delivery of the Ten Commandments; Sukkot, remembrance of the long pilgrimage through the desert to the land of Canaan; Hanukkah and the rebellion of the Maccabees against the oppressive regime of Antiochus Epiphanius; Purim, celebrating Esther, who with her daring saved her people from the massacre engineered by Haman; Tishá B'Av, perpetuating the memory of the destruction of Solomon's Temple, then also of the one Herod rebuilt. In our days, the Yom Hashoah. Last but foremost, Dana, the Hebrew! Who could imagine that thousands years later the language of sages and prophets would become the one of poets, writers and scientists!

With a millenary history that has become a living reality, the Jewish people have seen their culture deeply enriched by living together with other populations, thus creating a peculiar world of legends and traditions, literature, music, song, dance, humour and gastronomy. The Jewish heritage is so rich and immeasurable, Dana, that it has been considered a true civilisation.

The awareness of this rich legacy that not a few have tried to annihilate or, if not so much, are happy to diminish, is what sometimes leads the wronged Jew to a reaction of wounded pride. Such is what is said to have occurred to Benjamin Disraeli in the British Parliament, when attacked by the Irish leader Daniel O'Connell for his Jewish ancestry, and to whom he fought back: "Yes, I am a Jew, and when my illustrious opponent's ancestors were savage brutes on an unknown island, mine were priests in Solomon's temple."

Have I added even the tiniest bit to the many things that have been said about all this? I wish I had, Dana.

VIII

Jerusalem, the Cry!

Night. Slowly it leaves. It stops. Awaiting instructions. Plane glides, lifts tearing through the air. Flashing lights. Wheels coming back on, roaring. Then silence enveloping so many anonymous silhouettes, tied to the seats where they were placed. Who are they? What's taking them? For how long will they leave? Will they come back? Useless and futile questions to make you forget. You close your eyes, add darkness. Then you remember.

You left your parents, you understand? And your family and friends, do you know? And the country that nurtured you, the colour and smell of the land that made you, the serene and sinuous flow of the rivers, the salty taste of the sea where you bathed; the soft and gentle rumour of the pine forests, the tongue with which you let out your first wails, everything was left for you to erase, for you to let go, you comprehend? Knot after knot, you were opening a path, who know if towards pure inexistence, but it was all you wished. Because to emigrate is for one part of you to die, so that another may perhaps be born. You tried to mould yourself, you rejected the one they planned you to be, you ardently desired to believe, to speak, to live, not as you were taught to be, but under new emotions. You wanted to become the father of yourself. You traded your own father, do you understand? But your father gave you a bed to sleep on, and what do you do? But if leaving is to hurt, to harm, it will always be to arrive. What awaits you? If there is anyone, only the hand of an official who will write on you for the first time. And he will ask: what is your name? Prove it. And your father and mother, who are they? Do they have a name, your parents? As an answer, you will draw out a ream of crumpled papers which will give an answer about you and your parents. In a flash of a second you repeat yourself. You are so little.

Then throbs you the truth that the voice whispers, and does not haunt you. You're gone.

You arrive tired and heavy. You wish you had no bags to lift, to be born even again, with nothing to carry. But there is already an official who comes to you with a pile of sheets in his hand in which he has consecrated a single line to you. You are the one, yes, the one that the few letters sum up, then a scribble falls on you, a V, because you have arrived. Join to the right, those who are there. Wait. Then it's the scrawled paperwork that, just as you predicted, will talk about you, and you shut up.

They put money in your hand, it's a hundred liras, and a brief explosion bursts in you: what for? Keep it, it always comes in handy, even if it's for cigarettes, they say. The official's hand perforates yours with the dirty note, and to get rid of the other person's gesture, you take the folded paper and hide it from yourself. First vexation.

The small car is already on its way to Jerusalem.

It leaps and penetrates the night, night without stars or moon, it is really night. You and others sway, shake your heads, bodies approached. Until you arrive.

They give you a single room, and you shut yourself away from the fierce wind that howls and sweeps outside.

Again, the word that does not shake you invades you.

You emigrated.

No, Dana, I won't tell you about the time it was at the absorption centre that took me in. I soon understood that it was not for me, but I had to wait to hear from the university about the scholarship I had applied for. For that, I would have to have a few meetings. Once these were over, it didn't take long before the grant was granted.

The house I was looking for. For us. On the outskirts of the Hebrew University, with windows facing the rugged mountains where hour after hour the *muezzins* sang a repeated and sad call. There a room, and another, and the small room that we would fill with books and cuddles, with music and kisses.

Little by little, the first struggles began, to assure me an even minimal quality of life. First, the purchase of some furniture at Hamashbir, one of those stores where they sell a bit of everything: bed, table, stove, lamps, chairs, plus some other domestic utensils. Then there was the request for a telephone, followed by the promise that it would be installed soon. Finally, the search for information about what had to be done to get the container that would bring me the books, the records, the clothes.

But all of this, Dana, nothing, nothing weighed against the enormous challenge that soon I would have to face, because that was really serious. I'm talking about learning the language, Hebrew. The conditions of the scholarship were that it would last only one year. After that, I would have to be able to teach at the university, if the invitation came, or to take another direction, if not. But one thing was certain: I didn't know what "*álefe, bet, guímel*" was, and I had no time to lose. I enrolled in an *ulpan*, and there I followed an intensive course of Hebrew, with many, many heavy hours of daily study.

Learning. The alphabet. Basic words. First verbs, their conjugation. The beginning of minimal readings, serious difficulties in pronunciation. Some vocabulary of functional importance. We sometimes talked about the great complexity of the language. But you must permit me to say a little more on the subject. The truth is, and it did not take long for me to realise, as I felt it strongly in my skin, that I would face one of the greatest dramas of emigration: the progressive and voluntary detachment from the mother-tongue. And such distancing creating a vacuum that would become large, and filled in a rush, by injections of terms, rules and expressions, as if we were geese at the fair, growing fat fast, without commiseration.

Then, the mother tongue is being put away in the drawer of memory, thus causing a progressive and essential loss, the damage of a primordial heritage, the world of first letters, naive and small, that with us bloomed and grew, until it became a somewhat branched tree.

Do not see this as a lament, Dana, for I was telling myself for consolation that a new challenge awaited me: the study of that ancient and magical language of sages and prophets, miraculously brought to life. Its true knowledge, I knew, would remain for later. At the time, what was urgent was to forcefully penetrate the world that was opening up to me and whose main key was only one: the language, even if at the beginning it was expressed in a basic threshold, to serve daily life.

It wasn't long before they came to install my phone. At night, almost every night, I could hear you, Dana. The company would make the call itself – that's how the services worked in those days – and I would wait for the phone to ring to hear you. Flying through our affairs. About the progress of your master's degree. The *ulpan* and the difficulties in learning the language. The beginning of my thesis. The first advances. The apartment I had rented for us, and above all and repeatedly, the love that bound us and left a sour taste when the conversation ended.

I also told you, as I'm sure you will remember, of the walks in the old city, the visits to the museums, but no less of the pleasure of the study, the extraordinary library of the faculty and the archives full of old books in which I delighted to rummage.

So much, so many things, my God, that we talked about and laughed about with that childlike optimism that was ours, as if it were normal that everything should go straight on track, with effort and sweat, yes, but without alarm, without jolts. I was also confident that soon you would inform me of the end of your master's degree, and that I too, without much delay, would finish my thesis. Then it would be the beginning of new careers, and the world opening up to us with its range of promises. I loved you immensely, Dana; all dreams and projects were connected to your image, without it they would collapse for not being.

One day, I had a dream. We both laughed about it. The one about Magritte's *Château des Pyrénées*, the one that so often made me sit in front of it at the Israel Museum. There, I stood before the great rock topped by a closed castle of stone, suspended in a white and blue sky, where white and fluffy clouds floated in wonder at their own lightness. Below the sea, in the indifferent and soft curvature of a wave opening in kisses of foam.

Do you remember what I told you, Dana? It was me in my dream, a tiny black-billed bird born in the core of that rock, with no room to move. You laughed at my fantasy, as soon as I had started to say it. But the little bird ardently desired to free itself. With difficulty, as it moved, it began to prick, to prick the stone around it. Until, after unthinkable labour, it managed to open at the top of the castle a small vent to which it adjusted its round, blue eye. Then it saw. It was you, Dana, who regarding the undaunted rock and waiting with a restless gaze inquired, *"How? When?"*

It just so happened. The phone rang. The call for you, Dana, had just been made.

"Alan, Alan, I can't, I can't talk..."

And you cried, you cried, in gushes of pain. The cry!

"Dana, please, what is it, what happened?"

"Alan, my father... my father... died... my mother... and Lilucha... both very bad. Crash... The car crashed... Alan, I can't, I'm sorry, I can't take it..."

"Dana... please..." (sobs; silence)

"Dana!"

"Sorry, I can't. I must ring off."

Then it was like a cliff falling on me. I was crushed, rolled up, left like an inert object.

The phone again.

"Dana, I'll leave, I'll follow you, I don't want you alone."

"No, never, don't leave what you've already accomplished. No, Alan, I won't, no, no…"

"Dana, I can't go on without you. We will face together…"

"Alan, don't come, I beg you not to, I don't want you to come back at all. That's your great dream, you'd never forgive me."

"But tell me, Dana, what is it? How are they doing?"

"The mother, if she survives, will be paraplegic forever; Lilucha, with a skull fracture, among others."

You cried. We cried. The phone went dead.

I dropped into the nearby chair.

The next day, and two, and three days after, we spoke again, and your voice, Dana, fading, fading. Only reinvigorating to tell me that no, there was no way you'd accept me back.

I was insisting, repeating that I wanted you, but suddenly the receiver in my hand began to emit a thread of mournful, unison sound to let me know in its indifferent coldness that I was, would be, alone.

Sometime later, Dana, to another call from me, it was a male voice that answered to warn me, firmly and compassionately, "Dana cannot answer… asks you to understand… she will speak to you later."

IX

Lisbon Reinvented

One day. Back again. After years. Lisbon revisited. Once more, reinvented. Who knows if not the last. Pure morning. Where were you? I saw you in everyone that passed, yours modelling itself before me. I sought you, but you did not look at me. It was me who inquired and recreated you. You didn't even guess me, I almost gave up.

The hours of an illuminated blue May rose, and I dwelled on you, your presence. What if I called you? I did so. Then a rough, virile voice resounded. Cowardly, I hung up. Once more I tried it, then the same laxity. I will be back another time, I told myself, anticipating the likely laconic message that you, Dana, were not there. Nor would you be. For a time without measure. I returned. Suddenly, the line was cut.

I tried to calm down by walking in the street where I lived, where so many times we strolled together. Up to the house. There I saw it in its old vermilion. I counted the windows under its indifference. That's me. I could remember it with its nooks, one room, then another, and another, the corridor, at the end the living room, while I followed the footsteps of all those who went there, hidden and brief.

Below the Santana garden, a sombre stain of an austere grove of trees, expressionist in nature. In a monotonous litany, buses sipped and vomited people of timorous gestures, complacent to life's cheats. One or the other, more tied up in a great hurry, quickened pace, briefcase in hand. Young men in torn *jeans* and other slouches exchanged silences and remnants of drugs. Old men counting steps to the bank they were arriving at. In between, the slow and sleek rolling of some car, profiles of another cothurnus, still the rebellious roar of a motorbike reminding loudly to the others their destiny of little people, of nobody.

The sky of a childish blue, endless, silent. Soon, the return to the plain reality. On one side, the Paço da Rainha; on the other, the narrow streets leading to Bempostinha. Nearby, superb, the funereal mass of the institute where half of Lisbon had already seen its anatomised bodies. Leering in expectation, the funeral parlours. Above, in front of the pale façade of the old medical school, the pedestal where the gentle figure of the miraculous professor towered. Offering his hand, oblivious of the multiple tablets of gratitude for the cures made and others to come.

There was a gravestone nearby recalling those who were tortured in the Campo dos Mártires. Hangings, where could they have taken place? On the site of the octagonal green-glazed pastry shop? On the surrounding esplanade? In that lake where a paternal family of meek ducks sails, or rather on the lawn where the proud peacocks strut their stuff? No matter the place. In vain did I seek something of another that might be at hand. If only the warm and ancestral smell of a chestnut oven would blow...

Before I left, yet once more the thick and taciturn grove that for a moment the breeze loosened.

All around, the worked facies of the palaces of yesteryear, the wide sidewalks of a long-ago time. A whole scenario recalling in unison the unavoidable shortness of life.

Then the Lavra steps insinuated themselves. Unfolding in steps lowered and polished as an ancient floor. There the yellow funiculars, one carriage that rises, the other that falls, almost rubbing up against each other. Until, at the end, in Rua das Portas de Santo Antão. Darker and gloomier than before. Decrepit facades. A stench of gutters. It's around there that I came across bands of thugs, a flurry of brawlers stomping and exchanging blows in all directions. Roars and shouts of some who won the blow, others who squealed in pain. In the midst of it all, the horse guards arrived, their voices thundering, made even louder by the neighing of their horses. And as if they were determined to make their presence felt, riders and beasts stubbornly prowled through the crowd, leaving traces of blood in the street. So I saw them, under the neighing of the beasts, in a ribaldry, all of them needing that morning quarrel to break the daily round and delight the onlookers' muddled gaze. Then it was a guard who dragged and took with him two or three of the troublemakers, which led to cooling down the fight. But there still lingered a few thugs with the usual bravado, making the balance fight, until suddenly the scream was released. *Scoundrels, shit on them! They took Luís! Fucking cocksuckers! Fucking pussies!*

Luis. Was it really him, Luís? I still saw him, I thought it was him, already blind-eyed. Luís, Luís Vaz, Luís Vaz de Camões!* The same one I already knew from my primary school reading books, sometimes with so many illustrations, either saving himself and his manuscript in the sea, or reciting in the presence of the king. The one who one day was raised

---

* A plaque on the spot announces that on 16 June 1552, Luís Vaz de Camões was arrested there, for getting involved in a riot.

to the vertigo of the statue, left alone in the centre of the square, until he was finally relegated in an ostentatious tomb, in the company of Gama.

The guard had taken him away. So as I walked away, a wailing voice shouted to me from the top of a ventan:

"My errors, bad fortune, burning love for my doom they have conjured," while another already more conformed said, "Times change, wills change, the ways of being change, old credence grow strange, the whole world is made up of whirls of change…"

I was already on my way when a childish voice still intoned: "Barefoot, on the greenery Leonor goes to the fountain; goes handsome and insecure…" Then I heard no more, and I left.

Down below, the Coliseu, nicknamed Recreios. The one that had once seemed gigantic, now reduced to its human measure. Heavy. Stubby. An old circus where sleeping beasts obeyed the whistle of the whip, routine clowns, one rich, the others poor, encouraged easy laughter, cheap illusionists dropped silver coins from the noses of children, but then, oh God! made beautiful young women eclipse themselves from closed boxes under lock and key. In the mix, dwarves and critters, each one somersaulting in their own way, while blondes in minivestes framed that sad Sunday afternoon theatricality with smiles and wiggles.

Then the Estaus Palace. It was me, or it that sought me out? Old bastion of ill-faced turrets wanting to tell me "back here again in good spirits, huh?" But suddenly, it was already the placid theatre of white columns calming me with its serene, classic look, the face a little shy for such a sinister and pitiful past.

I still turned my back on the square of S Domingos and the church of foul memory, it was I who rebelled and I said to myself that only those who ignore it walk there, or those who don't care about the fateful history.

Next, Rocio. Glowing with light, it opened up to me like the kindest face of the city. The medieval and Moorish castle, the courtly space that it once was, at the top, far away. All around the square, rows of quiet houses with their mansards, in the provincial manner. In the centre, around a disremembered king perched on the top of a pedestal, green statues in baroque style, spurting out gushes of freshness. On the pavements, on the esplanades of the cafés, bunches of tourists sowed pinches of colour and modernity. But for the peace of those who wonder, there lies the theatre, in the background, attesting in its customary gentleness that the old Paço dos Estaus is no longer. Rocio. All of it a naive and contented smile, made of so many cosmetics.

I was looking for a place at Nicola. The old coffee house of Bocage, in the building where Eça lived, the Nicola – in its *Deco* geometrism, gracious and mild tone, where tradition and memory of some laughter has been generated – had always been one of my favourites. I took a look inside. The row of tables, all occupied, where I so often sat with Mário de Carvalho. A loyal guy, of unusual smoothness. Always, since his high school days, old Camões years. As time went by, he became a first-rate writer, and with what sobriety, without a hint of fuss. When the *Tales of the Seventh Sphere*, the first of the books, came out, I didn't even know he was the author. I received it in Israel, someone brought it to me. I read it with eagerness and I wondered if it was the same Mário of the short walks we used to take around the school, of the conversations and exchanges of books and impressions in which I always sensed that something was left unsaid.

At one of those tables we would sit for hours and hours, stirring our memories, recounting life, letting out a laugh.

But inside Nicola's there's no room. Everything's full. I went back to the esplanade. There was a table, next to which a single young woman. Blue eyes. She gave me a brief smile. Then a few short words: "May I?" "Oh, please, feel free!" Without waiting, the dialogue started. The banalities that feed the conversation: the charm of the city; the old neighbourhoods; the friendliness of the people and their smile; the beauty of Cascais, and Sintra, and Monserrate, and the sea, and the fish, oh! my God, such a wonderful country!

Her name was Suzane. Suzy, for friends. Sipping a colourful cocktail. It didn't take long for her to ramble on about New York, where she lived. She, her parents and Yoni, her brother, in an apartment in a numbered avenue. Barely seeing each other during the week. Everything's a rush.

"Only Friday night."

"For *shabbat*?"

"Are you Jewish too? Really?"

Then the conversation didn't follow a certain path. We jumped from Tel Aviv, where Suzy had family and friends, to the local Jewish community, how many Jews in Lisbon? Oh, so few! And in Portugal?... Really? Where are they from?

"You know, we are living not so far from the Portuguese Synagogue in Central Park West, the oldest Jewish congregation in the States, you know. When I was a child, my father took me several times to attend the Sephardic liturgy. So interesting!"

Then the conversation got a lot closer, it was about

Alfama. Then came the marranos, Belmonte, Castelo de Vide, Tomar, I don't know what else, until, after much history, we came to the conclusion that our grandparents were both from old Prussia.

It was when I was already getting tired of so much remembrance that a chalkhead cop frantically beeped, accompanied by much gesticulation, for passers-by to stop crossing the square. Soon other shrill, incessant whistles were blowing. The parade would begin. A motorcade. Here they came. Suzy found those cars amusing, at first very skinny, open and glowing in the sun, tires as thick as a fist. Then it was the turn of the more closed and circumspect cars, sporting a greater brio. She knew them all. A few Mercedes-Benz and BMW and the Rover, soon a greater automobile nobility, the Buick, the Nash, a Hudson or two, the Crysler and De Soto, and Packard, two Cadillacs, a white Rolls-Royce, convertible, which in its compassed and distinct roll was the one that most dragged the eye. And others. Until it was the turn of the motoring plebs, a mob of wheels hooting excitedly, they were the Deux Chevaux, the Renault 4, the old Beetles, a few tiny Austin and Simca, even an Iso Isetta, the tiny "egg" of the time, from which, with great difficulty, a large and painted clown playing concertina got out in the middle of the square.

The afternoon was turning pale. The vehicles paraded noiselessly and then faded away, as if nothing had happened before. The hissing of policemen could no longer be heard, their figures had disappeared. In a greater silence, it could be seen that at the end of the square another movement began to emerge. Made of moans and cries and other very sinister sounds. Strangely enough, the old theatre had lost its pale and soft face, to give way to the lugubrious grimace of the Paço dos Estaus. Then, from its mouth, a human reptile slowly began to grow and grow, beginning to snake through the vast square in a sluggish, cadenced stroll.

In the distance, as if chosen by a ray of sunlight, shone a silver crucifix to open the parade. Then, at a crawling pace, a ragged crowd came out, candles in hand. Some were weeping and wailing, others were affronting, many no longer in the mood for lamentation. Then came the turn of the sanbenitos, with large painted crosses, some with mitres on their heads. In the meantime, a fearful guard gesticulated, shouted in order to contain the frightened populace, soon beaten by the mere release of a blasphemy or a more acute cry. And the procession went on to the sound of a prayer mumbled in a single note*.

Mounted on mules was also appearing a throng of people, this already well-nourished, noble troop in velvety robes, clergymen and inquisitors.

Suddenly, my gaze flee to the opposite side of the square. There, where just before I had seen houses with closed windows, I now saw them framing faces adorned with ornaments, women with wide-open eyes and impatient haranguing, gathered to watch the parade in delight.

I looked for Suzy, whom I had forgotten for a moment, but Suzy was no longer there. Neither she nor anyone else on the esplanade. Not Nicola, nor the baroque statues pouring drizzle, nor the king on his pedestal. There only remained the dark serpent born from the mouth of the Estaus, made of a

---

* The events above concern the autos de fé during Inquisition, the building of the statue of king D. José, murder of king D. Carlos, a visit of Queen Elizabeth, speeches of Salazar and Caetano, who succeeded him as prime minister, made during the colonial war.

crushed and lowly people. There was still a cleric with a too-thin face, like an undertaker, who in his slow walk held up a red banner and cast a fiery glance at me, then I walked down the Rua Augusta. *Sale! Sale! Sale!* shouted the shop windows. I had been about to tell the people they had to protect themselves from the great queue that was approaching, but there was no longer a face, only fringes of hair covering it.

   I bumped into a dancer at points, all whiteness, half-sedated on a platform in the middle of the street, arms in the air. I touched her to tell her that the time was up, it was necessary to react. In return, I received a sleepy look begging me not to wake her. Finally, at the end of the street, a rectangle of brownish Tagus. Without understanding how, it was certain that the crawling queue born in the Estaus had already arrived there, and had crumbled to pieces. In its turn, it was a suffering crowd that, with shouts, mournful cries and a groaning voice, looked at so many miserable souls tied to wooden pillars. Then there were only sermons and shouts, fire and flames, smell of burnt flesh, while the prayer rumbled.

   But this did not last long enough, because the guard had already begun to chase the mob away, because the square had to be cleaned. Then came a lot of ox carts dragging thick and hard-working boulders. One and one more. They stood on top of each other. Half-naked, black men with shining chests and Herculean strength went about erecting the monument, while all around, people of decency and civility stood gazing at it. At one point, it was the young king who appeared, plus his minister. The latter, with a stony face and long, ringed hair, ordered him to climb up and stand on the pedestal. Then smile, he to the king said, and do no more. And fear not, for the earthquake will not come again. The little king did so. Quickly, he climbed the boulders with fearlessness. On the horse that was already there he took a seat, and remained there. All that was left was to put on his feathered helmet, wait for some creeping snakes around the royal statue, after which everyone was dyed in a green, hot, opaque rain.

After this, more and more came. Another king, this one already smiling and well-fed, but as he had nowhere to climb, there he was shot like a bull. Him and his young son.

A queen also appeared from the outside, looking like a princess, and as a rare mermaid got out of the water, she followed in a golden carriage. The populace pressed together to see her and manifest their joy, delightedly enjoying those brief moments of fantasy.

I could still see when, on one of the balconies of an old palace in the square, the grumpy, hard profile of an old teacher appeared, reminding the dulled people how much he knew and where he was going, which had always been his maxim. Nor could he be moved, unmerciful as he was, by the ships going to sea crowded with soldiers and returning crammed with coffins. The populace heard him and roared, until one day it shouted and didn't listen more. Then came another old professor, but soon he had to swallow his mournful voice, close his sour, aquiline look and vanish away.

Then, oh, my God, it was Suzy who suddenly appeared at my side, trembling and panting, and asked me why I had left her. Her face was sweaty, her eyes vacant and she smelled almost like burnt flesh. She begged me to take her away, at least to try to fly. She was able to do it, then I saw her leaving between gusts of a rushing wind, turned into a white seagull. I looked at myself. I was singed. I was listening to the turbulent waters of the river. Captive of the land, land of soft manners. I've forgotten everything. You too, Dana, I confess.